I Shall Love the Earl

I Shall Love the Earl

Laura A. Barnes

Laura A. Barnes

2019

First Printing: 2019

ISBN: 9781670914910

Laura A. Barnes

www.lauraabarnes.com

Cover Art by Cheeky Covers

Editor: Polgarus Studios

To: Grandma Ann
Who I spent many afternoons and Friday
evenings enjoying soap operas with. Thank you for
your unselfish love. I miss you.

Prologue

Rory Beckwith stood back in the shadows with his friend Sophia, watching the fiery redhead set down the Duke of Sheffield. If anybody had ever told Rory that he, Rory Beckwith, would fall in love at first sight, he would have called them a fool. But that was exactly what happened when he first set eyes upon Lady Dallis MacPherson. He couldn't say what it was about her that drew him to Dallis. Perhaps, it was her passionate speech to Sheffield, or the way Dallis held herself as she derided his arrogant behavior. All Rory knew was that he felt the connection deep in his soul.

He had yet to make her acquaintance, and now seemed like the ideal opportunity. Rory could play the hero and perhaps gain a dance. To hold such a beauty in his arms would be the perfect entertainment to help him forget about his troubles for a while. Even though his heart yearned for more, it would go no further.

Sophia burst into a fit of giggles, giving away their hiding place. Rory tried not to laugh himself. But the look on Sheffield's face when Lady Dallis described how she would hang him by his bollocks if he so much as spoke to her once more was too much for him to take. Dallis's Scottish brogue emphasized her threat. Rory gripped his side trying to hold onto his laughter, but failed.

Rory said, "I better rescue the lass, before the crowd inside notices this scene. I will return for our dance shortly."

Sophia couldn't stop giggling as she nodded. By now tears flowed from her eyes at her enjoyment.

Rory approached Lady Dallis. "Excuse me. May I escort you to your grandmother, miss?"

She gave him a thin smile. "Mmm, look, a gentleman in London. Observe and learn, Your Grace, on how a gentleman should treat a lady. Yes, you may, kind sir."

Rory held in his pleasure as the mere girl handed Sheffield a critique on his manners. He took hold of the young lady's hand and re-entered the ballroom. Sophia was forgotten as Rory became entranced by the beauty's spell. Lady Dallis's voice soaked inside him and made Rory feel as if he had finally come home.

Rory walked a few feet inside the ballroom and stopped near the windows behind a pillar. He turned slightly, still holding onto her hand. His need to keep touching her prevented him from following proper etiquette. He didn't want to incur her wrath and proceeded with caution.

"Are you well? Did Sheffield take advantage of you?"

"No. Are you going to?"

He stared into her eyes and noticed the teasing twinkle behind her question. His gaze continued to her lips where they were drawn into a mischievous grin. This woman was a minx sent to destroy all rational thought. Rory was speechless. He knew how he wanted to answer, but realized that reply would scare her away. He wanted to pull her into his arms and taste her sweet lips. Rory ached to hear her moan his name. Instead of acting on his desires, he behaved like a gentleman. He pulled them from behind the pillar and guided her near the other debutantes.

"No, that is not my intention."

He thought she murmured, "That is a shame."

Before he could ask, Dallis stopped near Lady Ratcliff and pulled her hand from his arm, stepping away. He felt her loss immensely.

"What is the meaning of this, Dallis? You left on the arm of a duke. Why are you returning with an earl?"

"Sheffield proved to be a scoundrel, Nanna. However, this earl proved to be a gentleman. Lord?"

"Lord Roderick Beckwith at your service."

Dallis had pretended that she didn't know her savior when, in fact, she had been aware of him since first setting eyes on him at the Havelock Ball. It was the first ball she'd attended this season, visiting her grandparents. Once she spotted Rory across the room, no other gentleman held her interest. It was as if fate threw Rory her way but played a cruel game by teasing Dallis with only glimpses of him. Finally, tonight she had grabbed his attention. Pure luck prompted the rescue from Sheffield. The duke was an infuriating man that she hoped she no longer had to deal with. However, the words Dallis spoke to the duke could be her downfall. One did not slander a duke without suffering repercussions. Dallis prayed that she was of no consequence to a man of Sheffield's rank—although in his search for a bride, Sheffield wouldn't want to be tarnished by any set-down from a lady he attempted to court.

She waited for her grandmother to introduce her to the earl. When her nanna only glared at her rescuer, Dallis took it upon herself.

"Lady Dallis MacPherson, and this is my grandmother, Lady Ratcliff."

"The boy already knows who I am, lass. Thank you, Beckwith, for returning my granddaughter to my side. I am sure my granddaughter only had a slight misunderstanding with the duke. Have a nice evening."

Her grandmother was dismissing the earl from their company. Dallis didn't understand why her nanna's manners were impolite. Since her arrival Dallis had been thrown at every titled gentleman in her path with the goal being the same of every other debutante present; to be courted with the result of a marriage contract. So why did Nanna rebuke Lord Beckwith's attention? When he was the only gentleman to whom she desired an introduction to. Dallis searched for him at every occasion hoping for this chance. Now her grandmother set out to ruin her opportunity at becoming better acquainted with Lord Beckwith.

"I had hoped to share the next dance with Lady Dallis."

"Her dance card is full for the evening, Lord Beckwith."

Dallis's grandmother had lied to the earl. She had one spot remaining, left open in hope. Now her hope offered and her grandmother refused him. Before Dallis voiced her objections, Lord Beckwith answered her grandmother.

"Perhaps, another time. I hope you enjoy your remaining time at the ball."

Dallis watched Roderick Beckwith walk away and return outside to the terrace. She'd lost her chance for the evening. Dallis turned to her grandmother to discuss the lie. Her nanna refused to meet her eyes.

"Why did you lie to Lord Beckwith? You are well aware that I had an open spot on my dance card."

"That spot is for anybody but Lord Beckwith."

"And why is that? He acted the perfect gentleman."

"Was that before or after your time spent alone behind the pillar?"

Dallis blushed, remembering when he hid them away. While nothing of significance happened, it wasn't without wishful thinking on her part.

Dallis defended Rory's actions even though she sensed there had been more to their private interlude. "That was for a brief moment in which Lord Beckwith inquired to my welfare. After I assured him, he immediately brought me to your side."

"I will not approve of Lord Beckwith calling on you."

"Why not?"

Before her grandmother could reply, her next dance partner approached. Dallis heard her grandmother sigh in relief at not having to discuss Lord Roderick Beckwith any further. However, Dallis wouldn't be so easily dismissed. Nor would her fascination of the earl stop. If anything, it enhanced her need to know more about him. What could be so damaging to his character to not be worthy enough to court her?

Dallis went through the motions of the dance, her thoughts straying to when Rory stepped out of the shadows to rescue her from Sheffield's arrogance. He represented every hero Dallis had ever read about in her romance novels. Lord Beckwith striding forward and whisking her away from the evil duke. However, it didn't escape her notice that he hid behind a potted plant with Lady Sophia Turlington. Were they having a secret rendezvous? Was that why her grandmother warned her away from him? Was he a shallow cad who toyed with ladies' affections?

Dallis had yet to be introduced to Lady Sophia. Every peer she had met adored the sweet-natured girl. Never an unkind word was ever spoken of her. The lady wasn't known to share her affections. Did Lady Sophia play the ton false? Was she one of those debutantes who used her charms freely? Dallis thought not. When Lord Beckwith and Lady Sophia emerged from their hiding spot, it didn't appear to be anything but friendship shared between the two. Not a trace of scandal surrounded them. Their garments were intact and not a hair out place. Their laughter at the duke's expense had caught her unaware. They appeared to take pleasure at her tirade. Also, Lady Sophia showed no sign of jealously when Lord Beckwith offered to escort Dallis away from Sheffield.

While Dallis had taken pleasure at finally capturing Lord Beckwith's attention, her mind still considered how she'd riled Sheffield's temper. Dallis overheard Lady Sophia's comment to Sheffield when they stepped through the doorway and realized she wasn't the only lady who disapproved of the duke's behavior. Lord Beckwith had escorted her away before she heard Sheffield's reaction to Sophia's enjoyment. When Lord Beckwith pulled her behind the pillar, she noticed the attraction shining from his eyes and knew he shared her feelings. He never released his hold, and her arm still tingled from his touch. Dallis tried to tease a reaction from Rory, but only caused him to end their time alone. She could only hope they would have more moments to come.

As her partner guided them through the dance, Dallis caught sight of Rory leaning against the very pillar they were hidden behind earlier. His gaze never once wavering. At every turn, their eyes would connect. The message his stare delivered was one she would never deny.

Chapter One

A couple of months later

Throughout the evening Rory watched Lady Dallis MacPherson twirled across the dance floor by one admirer after another. Each gentleman titled and rich above means, and who could afford her with a life of luxury. A privilege he could not. For he was broke beyond what his peers guessed but didn't know to the full extent. He could never dress her in the lovely gowns, furnish a house fit for a queen, or spoil her with jewels. No, Rory could only give Dallis his love. A precious gift, but not enough.

Still, his thoughts always wandered to the night he first made her acquaintance and the stare she returned his way. After her grandmother's refusal to let Dallis share a dance, he watched her from afar. When their eyes connected, he sent a silent message in which she returned. Her look shook Rory to the core. He relayed that Dallis was his and he would have her. She gave him a playful smile that said, *catch me if you can*. How he wanted to stride across the ballroom in that instant and stake his claim.

However, he needed a few more years to enhance his position. During that time, he couldn't expect Dallis to wait for him. She was young, and the kind of rare beauty sought after by so many. Dallis would only grow bitter toward him if he made an offer now. When they would have to scrape by for money to pay the shopkeepers, or share their meager funds with his mother and younger sister. No, it was best to sit in the shadows and suffer watching the men who were more worthy court her. No matter how much it tore at his heart, he would let her fly from his grasp—not that she was within his grasp to begin with. Yes, his friends Sidney and Sophia both urged him to court her, informing him of Lady Dallis's interest. They also warned of her grandmother's disapproval. He stood no chance. However, it didn't stop him from dreaming and admiring her from afar.

~~~~~

Dallis's glance kept straying toward Lord Roderick Beckwith standing in the shadows of the ballroom. She waited all evening for him to claim a dance, even leaving the last waltz of the evening open on her card. Still, he didn't approach her again, but she felt his gaze as she danced the evening away. With the ball finishing, her grandmother gave the last waltz away to Lord Fairmeadow who sought her attention, ending any chance of being held in Rory's arms.

She was under the impression from Lady Sidney and Lady Sophia that he admired her. Were they playing her false? Since she was new to town and didn't know anyone, she took what they spoke to be true. When the two ladies arrived for tea and invited her to a dinner party, she thought she'd made some friends. However, after the dinner party, her grandmother refused to allow Dallis to visit her new friends. The shocking courtship between Lady Sophia and the Duke of Sheffield unfolded and caused a scandal amongst the ton like no other. The ton deemed the duke, the man her grandmother wished Dallis to wed, a scoundrel. Dallis was also forbidden to associate with Sheffield anymore. Which didn't matter, for he would never ask for her hand in a dance again, because he married Lady Sophia a few weeks ago. The newlywed couple displayed their love openly. Which only caused more rumors to fill the gossiper's ears with their actions before they were wed.

When Dallis listened to the rumors, she would always sigh at the romantic story. She envied the couple and wished the same for herself. Nothing as scandalous, but she wished for a man to defy all tradition and sweep Dallis off her feet. She dreamed of a man to take her for himself and damn the consequences. Her grandmother was to blame. Dallis became caught in the drama, dreaming for it to be real just like she was the heroine from the romance novels she read to Nanna. In the latest romance she'd read, the hero defied all odds to make the heroine his, regardless of the circumstances.

When her dance partner swung her near the columns, Dallis's eyes again encountered Lord Beckwith staring at her. His gaze caused her to stumble over Lord Fairmeadow's feet. When she recovered, Rory had disappeared. Dallis searched the ballroom, trying to find him, while the marquess kept asking about her welfare. Lord Beckwith had left.

"Yes, I am well. I apologize for treading on your toes."

"No harm done, Lady Dallis."

By now the other dancers were colliding into them as they stood still. Dallis blushed at the attention. Lord Fairmeadow, a gentleman, escorted her off the dance floor and over to her grandmother. She felt awful for ruining their dance and accepted his offer for a ride in the park tomorrow afternoon. With her thoughts flustered, Dallis forgot to inform him she didn't actually *ride*. Her fear of horses kept her from riding a horse, to being a passenger in an open carriage, and Dallis only tolerated closed carriages because her grandmother's servants always guided the horses at a slow pace. It may take them twice as long to arrive at a destination, but at least Dallis remained calm throughout the ride. Tomorrow she would apologize once more to Lord Fairmeadow and suggest a walk in the park instead.

As the musicians packed away their instruments, and the guests began to leave the ball, Dallis searched for Rory before she left. Lord Beckwith always stood out in a crowd with his thick red hair that curled at his ears. Curls that she wanted to wrap around her fingers as she drew him close for a kiss. A kiss where … Dallis shook her head at where her thoughts led. Slowly turning, she found Lord Beckwith standing between the open doors to the terrace and regarding her with a look of desire. He'd never left.

When Lady Dallis turned, their gazes locked. Her mouth opened in surprise at his perusal. Rory took two steps forward. He forgot they stood in a ballroom filled with members of the ton. All he noticed was Dallis. Her strawberry blonde hair and emerald eyes. Her kissable red lips. Rory wanted to devour her mouth, staking his claim. As a man who desired to make her his.

Before he could act on his desire, Dallis's grandmother urged them to leave. The spell surrounding them broke, and once again Dallis was lost to him.

Chapter Two

Once again, he was there. This time it was during her walk with Lord Fairmeadow. When the marquess arrived for their ride, she confessed her fear of horses. Dallis was concerned that she would offend him. However, the gallant marquess elegantly held his arm out for them to walk. They were strolling through the park, conversing amicably, when she sensed Rory. Lord Fairmeadow stopped to talk to a couple and she noticed Lord Beckwith on a horse and watching her. Rory was stunning. He sat upon the steed in confidence, showing his control of the big beast with a firm hand on the reins. His regard was unwavering, and she felt flustered from his intense gaze. When Lord Fairmeadow guided them back along the path, Lord Beckwith tipped his hat. A warm blush spread across her cheeks at this open display of acknowledgement. In a daze, she completed the walk. Dallis must have displayed enough interest in the marquess, because Lord Fairmeadow inquired if he could call on her in a few days. However, she couldn't recall how she answered him. But if the smile he regarded her with, and the flowers that arrived the next day, were any indication, it must have been encouraging.

It wasn't only at the park. Over the next several weeks Lord Beckwith was in attendance at every gathering she attended. Not once did he attempt to speak with her. He only watched with his intense stare. Rory's eyes told Dallis how he felt. On each day, a variety of gentlemen packed her grandmother's parlor attempting to court her. She only paid them enough

attention to not offend them and pacify her nanna. The feelings Lord
Beckwith enticed in her soul kept Dallis from allowing any of the courtships
to go any further. Rory's glances entranced her and spoke volumes. Dallis
only needed some sign besides his gazes to send all the gentlemen away.
But when he never called or asked for her hand in a dance, her hopes were
diminishing away. With constant pressure from her grandparents to find a
groom for the season, she would soon have to give up her fascination with
the earl. If Rory didn't make a gesture soon, then Dallis would be left with
no choice but to make her own attempt. If he didn't respond, then and only
then, would she store her memories away and settle on another.

~~~~~~

Rory couldn't take his eyes off her. Dallis was an exquisite beauty
who captured his heart and wouldn't relinquish. Still, he held back. His
willpower weakened with each vision of her beauty. Tonight, his feet took
him closer, to hear the sweet melody of her voice. Dallis's glorious hair
swept atop her head in a bundle of curls. There were the usual strands loose
and teasing her neck. He wanted to kiss those strands and listen to her sighs.
Her Scottish brogue soothed Rory's soul. His friends kept urging him toward
her and he kept resisting.

Before he was aware where his feet led him, he stood behind her.
All he had to do was to reach out to brush his fingers across the length of her
exposed neck. To whisper in her ear his wish to kiss Dallis's delectable lips.
To wrap his arms around her middle and bring her flush against him. The
scent of fresh strawberries wafted from her hair and drew Rory even closer.
Dallis must have guessed his thoughts when she glanced over her shoulder
and encountered his gaze. Her eyes were green with flecks of gold waiting
for him. There was nothing to say or do, because Rory swore that she
deserved better. Dallis opened her mouth to respond to Rory's presence, but

her next dance partner interrupted before she could speak. Dallis turned her head, flashing the fool a smile, and allowed him to lead the way across the ballroom floor.

Once more, another chap claimed and whisked Dallis away from him. It didn't matter anyway, because Rory had stood there like a fool not speaking. They had spoken before, and Rory had even sat next to her at Sidney's masquerade dinner. But it wasn't enough, he craved more. Rory wanted to know everything about Dallis, her thoughts, her dreams, her likes and dislikes. He desired to tempt her with a passion only meant for them. Rory needed to kiss Dallis's lips and show her the love he wanted to give her.

Frustrated with seeing another gentleman lead her around the dance floor, he turned and stalked toward the terrace. Once outside, he let the cool breeze calm his soul. He leaned against the balustrade and spotted Dallis through the windows as her dance partner spun her around in circles. He only caught glimpses here and there, but it was enough. When the music ended, her partner escorted Dallis back to her grandmother and out of sight. Rory strode deeper into the shadows and rested amongst the columns. He was waiting for the damn ball to end so he could accompany his mother and sister home. He wouldn't end their enjoyment because of his own poor mood. They had little else in their life for happiness. Soon, he wouldn't know if he would be able to afford them this luxury. While he was still able to, he would put his feelings aside for them.

Dallis never lost sight of Rory as she danced. When he'd stood behind her, Dallis's heart fluttered rapidly. Dallis was positive he would seek her hand for a dance. As with every other ball, she kept a spot empty for him to sign. The need in his eyes drew her to him—a need that matched her own. Dallis knew he wouldn't speak, so she'd meant to put him on the spot and force him to ask her, only her next partner interrupted before she had a chance.

Well, not now, Lord Beckwith.

She saw him escape to the balcony alone. She pleaded an excuse to her grandmother about visiting the ladies' room. Instead her steps led her to the terrace and, reaching the doors, Dallis searched only to find the balcony empty. Walking farther into the darkness, she saw him standing beside a column. His stare drilling into her the closer Dallis drifted toward him. It spoke to stay away—which only drew her nearer. She didn't heed the warning.

She stopped a few inches from his brooding frame. "Are you following me, Lord Beckwith?"

"It would appear you are pursuing me, Lady Dallis. You are the one who followed me onto a darkened balcony. Are you looking for danger, or hoping it will find you?"

"Are you dangerous?"

"I could be."

"I do not believe you are. Now, back to my original question, my lord. Are you following me?"

"What makes you believe I am following you?"

"You appear at every invitation I accept, and every walk in the park. Wherever I am, you are near, staring at me with those intense eyes."

"You think I have intense eyes?"

"Yes, they are also dark, brooding, and hold an edge of danger."

"Mm, now you imagine I appear to hold a dangerous edge to myself."

"No, I suggested your stare did, not you."

"Oh, what a shame. I had hoped for dark and dangerous."

Dallis laughed. "You are trying to distract me from my original question."

Her laughter charmed his frustration. "Now I am a distraction. A fair one, I hope?"

"Are you going to answer me, Lord Beckwith?"

Rory pushed away from the column, coming to within a breath away from Dallis. Her sweetness engulfed him at their closeness. Only a small space of air separated his lips from hers. He shouldn't, but he did. He closed the gap and pressed his mouth to hers, catching her gasp. So sweet. Rory took another kiss, coaxing her lips to open. He kept his hands behind his back, afraid of his strong desire to hold her. He only wanted enough kisses to suppress his need for more. Just one taste would pacify him, something to hold onto in his memories. His tongue pressed until she opened for him. Rory invaded her mouth, taking no mercy, desire controlling his actions. He devoured Dallis, catching her moans as she responded with innocent strokes of her tongue.

Rory realized he must end this madness before he ruined her.

With his body protesting its disappointment, Rory stepped away. He would regret his next words, but they needed to be spoken. They didn't represent the man he was, but would give Dallis enough of a scare to stay away.

"Next time you follow me into the dark, my dear, you will find the danger you think I am not capable of. Go back to the simple gentlemen who court you, before you realize how dangerous I can be."

With that, he walked away and went to find a drink. The shock in her lovely eyes ate away at his gut. It was for the best. Rory didn't need her flirtation and come-kiss-me eyes. They were a temptation he must resist.

Dallis stood in the same spot for endless minutes. Between the shock of his kiss and the words he spoke, she didn't know what hurt more. That the kiss was nothing more than for his own pleasure, or the threat warning her away. Then she changed her mind, because Rory's kiss wasn't the action of a man *using* a woman. It was the kiss of a man who desired her and wanted more. To most ladies his words would have been a warning to stay away. To Dallis they only encouraged a desire to discover just how dangerous he could be.

Dallis walked into the ballroom a changed woman. She was no longer the debutante who waited for the gentleman she desired to court her. Now she was a woman who would chase the gentleman she desired. Lord Roderick Beckwith failed to notice that she was the dangerous one and would invade his life to show him. The smile on her face was one full of determination. Her eyes searched for him and found Rory at the bar in the corner, drinking one shot after another. Yes, she affected him. He would no longer be able to hide from her.

Now we shall see who follows whom, Lord Beckwith.

Chapter Three

The tables had been reversed. Everywhere Rory went Lady Dallis was there. His rides in the park, his visits to Lord Hartridge, every ball he escorted his mother and sister to, she was present. She even took it upon herself to befriend his sister. Of course, his friends Sidney and Sophia also aided Dallis to instigate herself into his life. And he thought they were his friends. Just because they were both happily married, they took it upon themselves to play matchmaker with him. Sidney was aware of his financial situation and urged him that love was stronger than money. In time he would repair his finances and all would be well. Rory wished that he had the same optimism, but the sense of despair kept him awake at night. Well, not the only thing. Sweet dreams of Dallis might play a part in his sleepless nights.

Those night made his days longer. Rory would wake grumpy and get more ill-tempered throughout the day. It was on one of those days that he encountered Lady Dallis and her grandmother. They were guests of his mother, having tea in the parlor. There she sat demurely on their meager furnishings, as comfortable as if she sat upon a throne. The upholstery had faded fast on the rag-tag chair and the legs were unbalanced. How she managed not to topple over amazed him. The shame of his family's standing soured his mood, watching the lady he wished for a bride sip her tea. She laughed with his sister on the antics of an earl they'd both danced with the evening before. The buffoon stepped on both of their toes and proceeded to try kissing them. The story angered him on two levels. One, as a brother who wanted to defend his sister's honor. Second, on the level of a besotted suitor jealous of another man attempting to stake a claim on Dallis.

"Don't you agree, Rory?" his sister asked.

"Agree on what?" he barked.

His mother immediately said, "Roderick Allan Beckwith, do not speak to your sister in those tones in the company of our guests."

"How I can, when none are present?" His sarcasm dripped amongst the ladies.

"Rory," his mother warned.

His quick temper hovered on the edge of exploding from the actions of Lord Phipps; who he would take care of later today when he visited his club. Also, it was frustrating having Dallis within arm's length and he couldn't act upon his desires. What made it worse was the smile on her face, full of mirth at his predicament. He realized Dallis knew what she did, and it was all done on purpose. Then there was his sister smirking as his mother reprimanded Rory in front of their guests as if he were a small toddler. It didn't set well with his ego.

"I am sorry, pet. What do you wish for my agreement on?" he gritted between his teeth with kindness.

His sister laughed. "Do you not agree that Lord Holdenburg would be perfect for Lady Dallis?"

It took everything in his willpower to agree. "Yes. A perfect gentleman. Lord Holdenburg should be honored for a chance at winning your hand."

And it was true, the earl acted the perfect gentleman with every lady of the ton. However, Rory knew the true character of Holdenburg. He was once a trusted friend, but now a sworn enemy. The man was nothing but a drunk and a gambler. Not to mention a scoundrel from whom he protected his sister. But to the ton's eye he was one of the popular set. Jealously gripped his gut once again. Lord Holdenburg stood a chance with Dallis that Rory never could. Even though the earl gambled heavily, he always came out the winner. While Rory's predicament could only be described as impoverished. Holdenburg was wealthy beyond any member of the ton. Lady Dallis could do no worse.

Dallis smiled serenely at his lie. "Why, such a lovely compliment, my lord."

"I speak only the truth, my lady."

Their eyes spoke volumes to each other. Each one sending a silent message. Her eyes telling him, *bull*. His saying, *over my dead body*. Dallis laughed and his shoulders relaxed at the mirth shining from her eyes. Rory should have known the very devil played against him.

"Excellent, I shall make introductions at this evening's ball," his mother replied.

Now his own mother worked against him. When the rest of the ladies discussed what Dallis should wear on her introduction to Lord Holdenburg, his frustration reached a new high. Soon the talk turned to hairstyle, jewelry, and the likes and dislikes of the gentleman. Dallis's excitement about this evening's festivities had him gripping the arms of the chair and shooting daggers toward the women. When his eyes encountered Dallis's grandmother, Lady Ratcliff, he was taken back. The lady's smile was devious and cunning. She arched her eyebrow, baiting him to interfere. He had been under the belief that the old lady thought him a fortune hunter. Was he mistaken? He gave her a small shake of his head, and she mouthed one word to him, shocking him in his seat.

Coward.

Coward? He wasn't a coward, was he? Rory glared back, but too late. Lady Ratcliff jumped into the conversation, urging Dallis to make a possible suit with Lord Holdenburg. Rory rose and left the room, not offering his excuses or thanking his mother's guests for their company. He could listen to no more or be under the mocking stare taunting him to prove her wrong. Lady Ratcliff wasn't mistaken, and that only made him more furious. He was a coward who wouldn't express his feelings to the beauty who claimed his heart. Not only was Rory a coward, but a weak one at that.

Out of the corner of her eye Dallis saw Rory leave. The other ladies hadn't noticed his departure. He was the other half of her soul, and she knew when he was no longer near. He left in anger. Dallis never meant to make him mad, only a bit jealous. Jealous enough to act. Instead, he let his frustration fuel his actions. The decision to leave. It didn't matter, she had a few more ploys to draw his attention. Rory would be in attendance tonight, because he always escorted his mother and Kathleen to every event.

Dallis would also seek the advice of her new friends, Lady Sidney and Lady Sophia. Her grandmother had forbidden accepting their offers of friendship. However, they were a connection to Rory that Dallis didn't want to relinquish. So with the help of her maid, she sent them missives and met with them without her grandmother's knowledge. She hated betraying her nanna, but knew deep in her heart she would understand. Nanna always loved a good romance with a happy ending. Sidney and Sophia were Rory's devoted friends, and they offered their support on winning Rory's love. When she arrived home, Dallis would send them her requests.

Then watch out, Lord Beckwith. Tonight you will dance with me whether you want to or not. Dallis returned her attention to the women discussing her clothing. She caught the eye of Rory's mother, who surprised her with a wink. Lady Beckwith continued on conversing with her grandmother as if the moment never happened. If Dallis wasn't mistaken, his mother granted her approval on pursuing her son.

After Dallis and Lady Ratcliff departed, Kathleen regarded her mother with a suspicious look. Her mother cleared the mess from tea and set the plates on the tray, aiding their ailing servant, Agnes. Their family was near the edge of destitute. The only servants they could afford was an aging butler, a cook, and one lady's maid who also did a bit of light housekeeping. Her mother and herself pitched in when necessary.

Rory worked hard to fill their coffers. Her father had been a gambler, betting on fights, horse races, card games; one after another, draining their savings. Mama didn't know the very fights her father bet on, her brother now fought in. Rory held a reputation with his fists that nobody could match, and his mind was just as swift. But as a research assistant for Lord Hartridge, it didn't pay well. It was not in favor of the ton's standards to gain employment, so everything Rory did to earn money for their welfare was done secretly. In the ton's eye, he helped Lord Hartridge as a hobby. In regard to his fighting, the contests were only witnessed by the degenerates of the ton too lost in their cups to care who fought. Many nights he returned home with his fists bloody and bruised. Never a mark to his face or body to indicate his activities. His hands were covered in gloves as fashion expected, so nobody saw the wounds. If Mama was aware, she turned a blind eye. Kathleen ached that her brother hurt himself to provide for them.

The rarity of her brother never went unnoticed as she met the gentlemen in society. No man could compare to Rory. She understood it would help their family tremendously if she were to find a husband to help support them. But she only wanted to marry for love, and not to a man like her father. So far, she had yet to encounter a gentleman to meet her standards.

"You are aware, Mama, Rory is madly in love with Lady Dallis?"

"Yes, Kathleen, I am well aware."

"Then why are your introducing her to Lord Holdenburg this evening?"

"To give your brother a kick in the rear to move forward."

"Mother, your language."

"Pshh,"

"He left instead of paying Dallis a bit of attention."

"Yes. However, throughout the entire tea, he never took his eyes off her. And he departed in a fit of jealously."

"Is it wise to bait his temper?"

Her mother smiled a secret smile. "If he is anything like your father, then it was just the right bait to entice him after her."

"What do you mean, Mama?"

"Trust me, my dear, after tonight your brother shall pursue Lady Dallis in a most scandalous nature."

"You are devious, Mother."

"Thank you, my dear. You remember that, for when your brother is married off, you are next."

Those were her mother's parting words as she lifted the tea tray and walked to the kitchen. Kathleen heard her talking to Agnes as they prepared dinner. Her mother would have to be more devious to see *her* settled. Because there wasn't a gentleman who drew Kathleen's attention enough for her to even think about getting married.

Chapter Four

Rory stormed into his club, searching for the reprobate who dared to kiss his sister and Lady Dallis. He found the earl bragging to his cronies of his exploits, and about the previous evening at a brothel attended by most the ton. Rory stopped and slugged him across the face. Lord Phipps slid to the floor in a heap, blood streaming from his nose. The red flow drenched his starched white shirt. The earl's friends scattered away from Rory's temper. He stooped and pulled the earl to his face with his cravat.

"If you ever so much as attempt to kiss my sister or Lady Dallis again, you will end up with more than a broken nose. Do I make myself clear?"

The earl nodded eagerly, his eyes wide agreeing to Rory's demands.

The whispered words of Rory's association with Lady Dallis would soon spread, the book filling with wagers about their relationship. Rory didn't care, he'd had his revenge and his temper started to cool.

As he rose and turned to leave, he encountered the smirks of the Duke of Sheffield and Lord Wildeburg, the husbands of Sidney and Sophia. They lifted their glasses as he passed and said, "Welcome to the club."

He stopped. "What the hell is that supposed to mean?"

"Oh, he has it bad," Wildeburg quipped.

"Worse than us, I declare." Sheffield agreed.

"Sod off, both of you."

"Allow us to buy you a drink, my friend. Won't you please join us in Sheffield's private room? You look like you could do with a couple."

Wildeburg urged him down the hallway into a private dining area. Leather bound chairs clustered around the fire and a bottle of scotch rested on the table. As he sat glaring at the men, Wilde poured him a drink and clinked his glass with his. Rory downed the whiskey in one swallow, causing the men to laugh more. Once Wilde topped his glass again, Rory relaxed in the chair. Punching Phipps and the alcohol relaxed his temperament.

"I always heard your fists were a force to be reckoned with," Wilde said.

"They are all I have at the moment."

"Perhaps we can be of assistance? Wilde has joined me in a business venture. Would you be interested?"

"Sorry, I have no coins for any investment."

"I can front you and take your deposit off the profits."

"Sheffield, I do not need your pity."

"I do not consider it to be a pity, Beckwith. I value your opinion. It is a tricky market I am unfamiliar with, but I feel there could be a huge profit in the venture. I respect your opinion from the discussions we share at Lord Hartridge's home and would like for you to be a partner."

"What is the venture?" Rory's curiosity was drawn.

"A shipment of silk, ivory, and wool."

Rory whistled his approval. He'd listened to discussions on importing these commodities. If he could invest, the profits would sustain his family for years to come. It would turn the state of their finances out of the red. Then his family would never have to worry about where their next coin came from. He decided to put aside his pride for his family's sake.

"Count me in. Only on agreement that interest is calculated on the return."

"Agreed." Sheffield nodded.

"Now, on to the real source of your temper. Lady Dallis MacPherson."

Rory remained quiet.

Both men laughed again and Wilde said, "Yes, Sheffield, he is doomed."

"You should be so lucky to have Lady Dallis's interest." Sheffield told him.

"You passed her over easy enough," said Rory

"Because Sophia held my heart. Anyway, she was not interested. Her heart lay with another."

"How would you know?"

"She told me on the day we took a walk. The same day my wife laid her head on your shoulder."

Rory cringed, remembering that day. It was the morning after he pummeled Sheffield in a fit of jealously and rage. Still, now he knew— Dallis loved another, and he didn't stand a chance.

"Then my pursuit of her would be hopeless."

"I always heard you hit your opponents in the head. However it would appear you must have been hit in the head too many times yourself."

"Beckwith, she is in love with *you*," Wilde helped him with the confusion, playing the peacemaker.

Rory sat in confusion. Dallis loved him? Was it possible? He thought she might have held an attraction toward him, but never imagined it could be love. Did this change everything?

"Sorry, Sheffield," Rory muttered.

"I deserved it. For every reason you landed your fists on my face, it was justified."

"What is your plan?" asked Wilde.

"I have none. During their visit this afternoon for tea, my mother brought up an introduction between Lord Holdenburg and Lady Dallis. Lady Ratcliff agreed that it would be an excellent match."

Both men looked grim. Every lady who encountered Holdenburg's charms was drawn under his spell never to return. Rory's sister was the only lady immune to the scoundrel's charm. Holdenburg was a close friend of their family. When they'd attended school at Eton, Rory ran with him and got into more trouble than their mothers desired. His family also held ties to Ireland. After Wildeburg married Sidney Hartridge, Holdenburg moved into the slot as the most sought-after scoundrel in the ton. His stories were legendary in their own right. That was the main source of Rory's anger. He knew that as soon as the introductions were made between Dallis and Holdenburg, Rory would pale in her eyes. She would no longer be interested in the possible danger of Rory Beckwith, instead she would be tempted by the smooth charm of Lord Devon Holdenburg.

Rory acknowledged their expressions. "My sentiments exactly."

"Perhaps Sidney can assist?" Wilde suggested.

"With one of her love experiments?" Rory scoffed.

"Yes, except for now she is referring to them as love matches. After Sheffield and Sophia got married, Sidney now calls herself a matchmaker."

"She was *not* involved in our relationship," Sheffield stated.

"Wasn't she, my friend? Who do you think assisted Belle? Also, the masquerade dinner was her idea."

"So, I have her to blame for almost losing Phee."

Rory watched as they argued about Sheffield's bizarre courtship to Sophia. It caused the biggest scandal the ton had ever seen. Any other couple would have been ostracized to the country. However, the sweet nature of Sophia and the devotion displayed by Sheffield endeared them to the ton. The sweetest soul to mankind brought a scoundrel to heel. How his friend softened such a hardened bastard remained a mystery. Even his own relationship with Sheffield had changed. At one time the duke thought himself so far above Rory and barely tolerated him, and now Sheffield considered him an equal. All due to Sophia. Rory sometimes still wanted to beat to a pulp both of the men who sat before him, because of their actions toward the two women who were like sisters to him. One of the gentleman he did. Still, they were not lightened in his eyes. They would have to continue to treat the women with love for him to soften. Until then he would respect his friends' decisions and be willing to change his mind in the time to come.

Rory rose. "Give your ladies my love and please do not interfere. For now, it would be in Lady Dallis's best interest to become acquainted with Lord Holdenburg."

"Yes ... well, you see, *you* have already interfered in your relationship with Lady Dallis. By now bets are being made in that regard, probably at this moment," Sheffield said.

"How so?"

"Your punch to Lord Phipps?" Wilde reminded him.

Damn. Rory wanted to punch himself for such an idiot move. Now his mistake would tie his name to Dallis for this season and all to come, especially if nobody offered for her hand. When Rory had mentioned Dallis's name with the punch, he'd declared his intention toward the lady. If he would have only said his sister's name, they would understand he defended Kathleen's honor. He slouched back in the chair, drinking the whiskey that Sheffield refilled for him.

He continued to sit and drink all afternoon with Sheffield and Wildeburg as they offered advice on his newfound dilemma. The other gentlemen didn't drink. To their dismay he finished the bottle, and with a wave he dismissed their offer to help him home.

Before he went anywhere though, he needed to offer his apologies to the lady he offended. Once he sobered, he would realize he only made matters worse.

Chapter Five

Dallis heard the pounding on the door and realized that for some reason Shaw wasn't going to answer the caller. Even though it was highly improper, Dallis opened the door herself. She stood in surprise at who stood on her doorstep. Lord Roderick Beckwith swayed back and forth, trying to fight for his balance. His eyes glazed over as his lips pulled into a lopsided smile.

"Yous is sooooo betiful."

He was drunk. The ever-proper, keeping his temper in a tight control, protective Rory Beckwith, was blazing drunk. He reached out to wrap his finger around a stray curl.

"Soooo soft. Knew wods be."

Rory's touch stilled Dallis from helping him stand. The gentle caress caught her unaware. His thumb brushed across the loose strand. Rory continued to sway and soon lost his balance. He fell into the doorjamb, where he decided to lean. When Dallis didn't respond to Rory, he took his touch one step further and brushed his thumb across her lips. The jolt propelled Dallis closer to him, her mouth opening at his touch.

"Soft engf to kiss."

Dallis didn't know how to react. Rory was finally near and touching her. Her body took over, responding to his need. Her tongue slowly slid out to lick his thumb. At her reaction, he groaned and pulled her into his arms.

"See, I tolds you I's dangerous."

Rory's lips devoured hers passionately, exploding her senses. His mouth pulling kiss after kiss from her soul, while his hands dived into her hair causing her hair pins to scatter across the foyer. As he sensed her desire, the kiss turned more urgent. Everything she ever read about was coming true at this moment. Still, Dallis held back from responding due to her naivety. Until he groaned and tightened his embrace, giving her the encouragement to return his kiss and match him stroke for stroke.

"We thought this might be your next destination. C'mon mate, before the neighbors catch sight of your stupidity. I told you, Sheffield, that he would go to her."

Sheffield and Wildeburg pulled Rory away from Dallis. Her face flamed with embarrassment to be caught so intimately in Rory's embrace. Dallis held her cheeks as Wildeburg led him away.

"Sorrysss Dallis," Rory called out.

"For the kiss?" she whispered.

Sheffield answered for him. "No, my dear, for another matter. I am working to quell that problem. But you should be aware that he defended your honor at the club today with Lord Phipps."

"Defended, how?"

"By a bloody punch to the nose."

"Oh. More to add to my embarrassment."

"I am afraid so. Do you remember our conversation in the park?"

"Yes."

"If it is any comfort, you are not the only one suffering from love."

"Then why does he ignore me?"

"Pride, my dear Dallis. A man's greatest downfall in life."

"Pshh."

"My sentiments exactly."

"Thank you, Sheffield."

"Anything for a friend. Will we see you at the Sambourne Ball?"

"Yes, I am very excited. Lady Beckwith offered to introduce me to Lord Holdenburg."

"So I have heard. Another reason for our acquaintance's inebriation."

Dallis smiled. Rory's display of drunken affection proved he was jealous. Was he jealous enough to stop the courtship her grandmother proposed? If not, his actions this afternoon secured that he must court her or ruin her reputation. They could have explained away the punch, but the kiss held the most damage. Dallis knew her grandmother's neighbors watched them. There wasn't an activity in the neighborhood they didn't observe.

"Give Sophia my love."

"Will do. Please save me a dance this evening. We might as well make the bloke so bloody jealous that he will become a pup at your feet, begging for a treat."

Dallis closed the door as Sheffield entered his carriage. She leaned against the paneling, her smile growing wider, realizing she had Rory right where she wanted him. Her smile turned to astonishment as she remembered the taste of him on her lips. She pressed her fingers to her mouth. Would he recall their kiss after his drunkenness wore off? If not, she would be sure to refresh his memory.

~~~~~~

Rory rolled over on the bed, moaning his discomfort. With his eyes still closed he waved at the annoying disturbance. His forehead felt like tiny hammers were attacking his skull. Rory became wide awake when a hand swatted him upside the head.

"Ouch."

"Wake up, Rory Beckwith."

Rory wondered why the hell Sidney was in his private bedchamber. If Wildeburg realized where she stood, he would be a goner. He didn't want to fight her husband. Especially now with this hangover he suffered from.

"Leave, Sidney," he muttered.

"Leave? This is my home, Rory, and you are the one who needs to leave."

"What?" he asked, opening his eyes. He lay on a bed covered in luxury. The hangings on the wall were velvet, and the drapes were made from the finest Japanese silk money could buy. The furnishings were of quality craftsmanship. Not the beaten chest that rested in his bedroom. He moaned, holding his head, the memories of the afternoon spilling forth.

"Are you remembering your foolishness?"

"How bad was it?"

"Real bad."

"I'm a fool?"

"Yes, you made a fool of yourself, but in the most endearing way."

"How so?"

"Well, from what Wilde described and Sheffield confirmed, you kissed Lady Dallis in broad daylight on her front stoop."

He didn't need Sidney to remind him of *that*. The memories had flashed to the front of his mind as soon as he awoke. Probably because he dreamed of her. How Dallis's gentle lips, unsure of how to kiss, pressed to his as he'd coaxed her to follow his lead. Even as drunk as Rory had been, he would never forget their kiss. Not only the kiss, but the sensation of her body crushed to him. Dallis was soft and curvaceous in all the right places. He wondered what hidden delights were under her dress.

"Damn."

"Watch your language in my home."

"Sorry, Sid. I tried to stay away."

When Rory rose to the edge of the bed, Sidney sat next to him.

"Why are you staying away from her? Sophia told me about your feelings for Lady Dallis."

"Sid, you know how broke I am. I cannot afford a bride for at least a few more years. It would not be fair to ask her to wait, or to wed her and subject Dallis to the poverty Mama and Kathleen have endured since father died."

"I understand where you think it might matter. However, when you are lucky enough to have found a woman to love you through the good times and bad, you cannot let her escape from your grasp."

"Easy for you to say."

"Rory, Dallis cares for you."

"How? We have barely spoken."

"The same way you care for her. You two share an attraction where no words are needed."

"It doesn't matter. Mama is introducing her to Lord Holdenburg this evening."

Sid whistled. "Then you don't stand a chance anymore. He is more dangerous than my Wilde."

Rory nodded.

"Well then, we shall do an experiment to see if Lady Dallis is—"

"No! No research, no experiments, and neither Dallis nor myself will be one of your test subjects. Nothing. Lady Dallis will not be a pawn in your science."

"Humph."

"Sidney, I am serious."

Sidney rose and walked to the door. Rory had offended her by not taking up the offer to help bring him happiness. She thought, *Why, just look at how I helped Sophia and Sheffield find love.* Sidney knew in her heart she could make Rory and Dallis just as happy.

Well, Rory doesn't have to know about my involvement. Lady Dallis had called on her today asking for advice. Also, Rory's mama wanted her aid in bringing these two young loves together.

"Very well, Rory. Your mother has sent over a change of clothes for this evening's ball with a message to attend so that you can escort them home. I sent a reply informing her of your business meeting with Wilde and Sheffield. She understood completely. Sheffield and Sophia have agreed to escort your mother and Kathleen to the ball."

"Thank you, Sid. Sorry," he mumbled. Rory was ashamed for speaking to her so harshly when Sidney had covered his misdeed and offered her help.

"We are leaving in half an hour." Sidney said, closing the door.

Rory sighed and dropped his head into his hands. He'd blown it on so many levels today with all the women in his life. The only one he managed not to offend was his friend, Sophia. The evening was still young though. Rory was sure he would manage it before the night was through. Rory needed to sober up quick before he stepped foot at the Sambourne Ball. By now talk would have spread about his antics this afternoon. The fight was bad enough. The kiss confirmed he must now court Lady Dallis. Or else the only callers she would entertain were gentlemen who would have devious intentions. Not that *his* actions toward the lady were any more innocent. He knew the plan for this evening was for his mother to introduce Dallis to Lord Holdenburg. Perhaps, if Rory talked Holdenburg into pressing his courtship with Lady Dallis, then Rory could bow out gracefully.

Then the ton would realize he'd stepped down in order for Lady Dallis to find happiness with Lord Holdenburg.

As Rory dressed, his thoughts strayed to Dallis. She'd stood with a bewildered look on her face as he pulled her into an embrace, her eyes wide as his mouth invaded hers. Her gentle exploration as his mouth demanded more. Could Rory step back while another man made Dallis his? Could he keep a tight rein on his jealously? Did he even want to try? If this business deal with Sheffield succeeded, then he could offer Dallis the moon and all the stars in the galaxy.

Maybe, tonight, he would request permission for a dance.

Chapter Six

Another ball was almost to an end, and still Dallis had received no request for a dance from Rory. Dallis's thoughts drifted back to when he had arrived. The ballroom quieted when Rory walked in with Noah and Sidney Wildeburg. He strolled to his mother's side, bending to kiss her cheek. Then the ballroom came to life once more, with hushed whispers and rumors spreading. Still, he never once acknowledged Dallis. After all, the gossip surrounding them was sprinkled with vicious innuendos. How dare he ruin her reputation for the sake of a drunken kiss? She deserved better. When Lady Beckwith introduced her to Lord Holdenburg, Dallis became enamored. He wasn't Rory, but a close second. The lord exuded charm in abundance, dancing with her twice, and supplying the gossip mongers with more feed. Not only did two men wish for her affection, now it drove all the other gentleman toward her. Their range of requests went from asking for her hand in a dance, or a walk around the ballroom, to escorting Dallis to dinner and the usual offer of a glass of punch. Her dance card filled quickly for the evening, and her poor toes throbbed from the unwanted attention.

The only gentleman she wanted to dance with refused to ask. Still, as usual, she held a spot for him. What frustrated Dallis the most was that Rory offered every other wallflower sitting by the wall a twirl around the ballroom floor. Everybody but her. During her dance with Sheffield, Rory glared at them from across the room. Sheffield laughed as he noticed, brushing hair off her cheek to anger Rory even more. Which it did. Rory started toward them and Sheffield swung her into a crowd of dancers so that they were lost from Rory's view. Sheffield told her the chap deserved it, and he enjoyed the sweet payback. Dallis wasn't as sure as everybody else this evening. They'd planned to have Sheffield dance with Dallis, while Sophia persuaded Rory into dancing with her. Then Sheffield would interrupt them and switch partners. However, the plan didn't work. Rory refused to dance with Sophia.

The musicians signaled the last dance of the evening with the opening notes of a waltz. The soulful music drifted into her, pulling at her need to be in Rory's arms. She lifted her head to meet his gaze. Rory stood a few feet away. When their eyes locked, the notes hit a melody, drawing them together. He held his hand out and she slid her palm into his. Rory swept Dallis into the dance, their bodies moving as one across the floor.

Until now, he had resisted dancing with Dallis. But the pull of music from the orchestra urged him to her side. The sadness radiating off her touched his soul. The need to hold Dallis as they danced was stronger than the need to deny her. Rory couldn't do that again, no matter how much he needed. Each turn, their bodies pressed closer. His hand wrapped around her waist, gripping tight with a need for more. Dallis's hand nestled in his suggested a trust he didn't deserve. Her other hand trembled on his shoulder, revealing her desire. Rory squeezed her hip, relaying how he shared the same emotion. When her head lifted and Dallis's eyes confirmed what he sensed, he felt ten feet tall.

When the dance ended, they stood in the middle of the dance floor. The other dancers separated and wandered away. Still they stood with Rory holding Dallis in his arms. Their eyes locked in an unspoken message they both understood. Rory silently told Dallis that he would pursue her until he caught her. Her reply was that she waited with open arms.

When Rory became aware that all the eyes in the ballroom were fastened on them, he released Dallis and stepped away. He bowed and thanked her for the dance. Then he walked away yet again, collecting his mother and sister. Before he left, he stopped in the doorway with one last glance in her direction. His sensuous eyes held hers in a trance—then abruptly turned to a glare before he stormed away.

His glare confused Dallis. Then she understood when Lord Holdenburg lifted her hand to rest on his arm. The earl offered to return Dallis to her grandmother. He spoke on how some members of the ton held such deplorable manners, and Holdenburg offered apologies for the behavior of Lord Beckwith. Then his conversation swiftly turned to his delight on making her acquaintance and expressed his wishes to call on her. Dallis agreed, realizing it was useless to expect otherwise from Rory.

Dallis came to a decision. Even though Rory had danced with her this evening, he'd still subjected her to the ton's gossip, the waltz only amplifying the whispers of his regard toward her. If he didn't want her ruined, he should have *asked* for a dance, not claimed one that he didn't sign his name for. Even though she held the space on her card open for him and him only. From now on, no more. If he wouldn't pay her the respect she deserved, then she would pine for him no longer. Rory was either man enough to stake his claim, or he *was* the coward she didn't have him pegged to be. Either way, it was time she allowed the other gentlemen of the ton to court her. Starting with Lord Holdenburg. There was something devilish about him that intrigued her. It might even be entertaining to have a charming rogue court her.

As Rory waited for his mother and Kathleen to gather their wraps, he stood in the shadows watching Lord Holdenburg escorting Dallis back to her grandmother. The scoundrel had her laughing while he held her hand. Rory gripped his hat in his hand, ruining the trim. How could she dance like heaven in his arms one moment, and the next laugh over a scoundrel's charms? Rory realized he'd blundered his chances yet again this evening. With all good intentions to lay claim to her, he froze when he watched gentleman after gentleman claim Dallis's hand for a dance. All his doubts and insecurities had floated to the surface until he danced with her. Rory wanted more. But he couldn't act on his intentions, because all eyes had followed them to see what course of action he would take. And like always, he did nothing. Dallis had him twisted inside and out and he didn't understand what to do.

Tomorrow he would make amends. He would send her flowers and take her for a walk in the park. Perhaps, like Sophia, Dallis liked to feed the ducks.

Chapter Seven

"Ahh, brother dear, tsk, tsk, tsk."

"What now, pet?" Rory asked, studying the ledgers.

"Mama is so disappointed in you. This is worse than the time you punched old Lord Cranky."

Rory threw down the quill and rocked back on his chair. It was useless anyway to figure his finances. His assets were tight and would remain that way until he could draw a steady profit. Even with his nightly fights, the shopkeepers would threaten to throw him in debtor's prison any day now. This morning, he'd decided to accept Sheffield's loan and join the investment opportunity. Rory hoped for a profit, and if not they would have to sell the townhome. He thought maybe his mother had heard of their dire situations. Oh, she was aware they were low on funds, but not how desperate they were. But from the knowing smile on his sister's face, rather than her being distraught, Rory realized his mother was at least unaware yet of their need for coin.

"Mama is never unhappy with me. Are you certain you have not mistaken me for yourself?"

"I am an angel compared to you today."

"Humph, an angel my arse."

"Now vulgar language in front of a lady, your offenses are piling high, my brother. Are you sure you want to add to them?"

"Spill."

Kathleen ticked off her fingers all of his indiscretions as she listed them. "First, there is the bloody nose you gave Lord Phipps for trying to kiss Lady Dallis and myself. Even though I think the punch was more for Dallis than for me, but thank you nonetheless for including my welfare in the punch. I would have done it myself, but Mama says a lady should never display any acts of violence. Second, there is a rumor spreading that you were drunk and kissed Lady Dallis on her doorstep in a most vulgar fashion. However, I disagree. I think it sounds romantic. With you sweeping Dallis off her feet in a passionate embrace and her falling into your arms succumbing to your desire. Third, there was the dance you shared with Dallis at the Sambourne Ball. If that was not an intimate moment for the ton to view, then I do not know what is. And to end all ends of your disappointments, there is the matter that it has been three days since the ball and not once have you paid a visit to Lady Dallis. Nothing. No afternoon tea, no walks in the park, no flowers, and not a single effort to court her. You have ruined Lady Dallis, yet you take no means to right your wrongs. Meanwhile, Lord Holdenburg has stepped forward to lay claim to Dallis's hand."

His sister's long-winded speech on his ungentlemanly behavior sat heavy in his gut. Rory realized how the impact of his three-day absence would affect Dallis. It wasn't as if he didn't care. It was the complete opposite, he cared too much. To be honest, his depth of emotions for Dallis scared him. The feelings she invoked in him were more powerful than anything he'd ever experienced. One glance from Dallis set him afire. Ultimately his pride stood in the way. Rory wanted to court her as a man who was financially sound. Not one who called on his love without a coin to his name.

Did the women who surrounded him not understand? For the last few days, when he visited Lord Hartridge to help him with his research, Sidney and Sophia bombarded him, offering advice on how to pursue Dallis. When he rejected their advice, they harassed him by calling him all sorts of a fool for not following his heart. Finally, he'd left and hadn't returned since. Lord Hartridge took pity and told him to return later when the girls wouldn't be there. Since Lord Hartridge hadn't contacted him, Rory knew they laid in wait. Now he couldn't even enjoy the one job he took pleasure in without being subjected to two opinionated women. Nay, they were his friends.

"Well?"

"Well what, Sis?"

"Are you going to call on Dallis?"

"No."

"Why not?"

"Mind your own business."

"You are my business at the moment."

"Perhaps I should mention to Mama the need for you to find a husband this season?"

"You would not dare."

"Wouldn't I?"

Kathleen fumed in her seat at the threat Rory sent in her direction. He wouldn't dare. It was empty-handed, only spoken so that she would leave him alone. But no longer. Rory deserved happiness for the weight he'd carried on his shoulders the last few years. And Dallis was just the woman to ease his burden.

"Rory, you deserve happiness. Dallis is the lady who makes your heart beat. I have seen the change in you since she arrived in town. Your step is lighter, you smile when you watch her, and a tenderness softens your eyes when she is near. Why are you not pursing her, Rory?"

"You know why."

"For a foolish reason. None of that will matter with her."

"This is something you will never understand."

Kathleen rose from her seat and paused at the doorway. "Do not let pride stand in your way of happiness. A lady of Dallis's quality is a rarity. A once in a lifetime chance. Go to her before the scoundrel Lord Holdenburg whisks her away."

Rory stared at the vacant doorway and let her words sink into his soul. Pride was a damnable emotion for a man. If a man didn't have pride, then he was weak and succumbed to vices out of his control. His father was a perfect example. However, in some men pride was their domineering ability to have everybody succumb to them. Rory was neither of those men. Somewhere in the middle, he wavered. He'd watched men for whom pride was their fall. Sheffield and Wildeburg were perfect examples. When they thought they'd lost the love that made them whole, they sat their pride on a shelf to prove to the women they loved that they were men who couldn't live without them. Each man in their own right still kept their pride, but learned to display it in a different nature.

But they were two men who weren't in a financial mess.

Rory couldn't by all rights continue with this madness. He didn't eat or sleep, and Dallis consumed every one of his thoughts. She deserved better than the treatment he displayed toward her. He owed her an apology and one to her grandmother for bringing shame on their family. Not only them, but he owed one to his mother and sister too. Rory's actions affected them just as deeply, if not more so. But by god if he would apologize to Lord Phipps. The bloke deserved the punch and was lucky he didn't get more.

~~~~~~

Dallis stared out the window, watching the wind and rain pelting the earth. The trees swayed with each burst of the storm. Huge raindrops soaked the pebbled streets. The wind howled causing the shutters to bang against the house. Her grandmother's servants hadn't secured them before the storm rushed upon them. Dallis enjoyed watching Mother Nature in action. Dallis always felt secure in a storm, never frightened like most girls she knew. She hated her time at school when the girls would whine in fear. Sometimes Dallis would sneak outside to stand in the storm. She would let the water beat down upon her, lifting her face to the sky. Her grandmother would scold her if Dallis attempted such an act now.

The storm matched her mood this afternoon. Dallis wished she could howl along, for she was beyond frustrated. Rory never paid her a visit over the last three days. Every place Dallis visited she heard the whispers of her name associated with his. The pitying looks she received ended with her glaring at them in return. The only consolation was that Lord Holdenburg called on her, which encouraged the other gentlemen to pursue her. However, the difference was that they pretended to be courting when really they wanted to kiss and grope her when nobody glanced in their direction. All thanks to Lord Roderick Beckwith, she was now labeled as the wallflower to steal away into the garden with. Everyone connected to Rory offered their apologies for his behavior. Everyone but him.

The rain wasn't the only thing that drew her attention. The man standing across the street and watching her through the window, huddled in his coat, made her stare. She recognized Rory, and was past caring if he would arrive. The damage had already been done. Any word that passed through his lips would mean nothing to her. When her gaze connected with his, he straightened and walked toward her front door. It didn't matter, for she no longer cared that he'd finally decided to visit. When Shaw announced Rory, she would plead a headache and send him on his way.

"Come from the window, Dallis dear, and read to me for a spell."

Dallis turned and smiled at her grandmother. Her nanna meant the world to her. She always made her feel special with various degrees of affection. Her granny demanded nothing from her, whether it be how she acted, or what her interests were. Nanna loved Dallis for who she was, not what was expected of her. For that, her grandmother would always hold a special place in Dallis's heart.

Before she sat with the book, she wrapped a stole around her grandmother's shoulders. Whenever Dallis read to her, Nanna would fall asleep. Dallis settled in the chair and opened the newest romance novel. Her grandmother used to read these novels to her when Dallis was very young. She always dreamt of meeting her soul mate and falling in a deep, abiding love that would last an eternity. Ever since her grandmother's eyesight failed, Dallis read the novels. Each one filled with romance and angst, but they all ended with the hero and heroine professing their undying love and living happily ever after.

After reading a couple of pages, Shaw interrupted informing them of a guest. When Dallis inquired to the guest's name—although she knew—she sent a refusal pleading sickness. When she resumed reading the novel, Dallis saw her granny's eyes narrow in suspicion. Still she kept on narrating the novel. When Shaw didn't return, Dallis assumed Lord Beckwith accepted her excuse and left. She continued reading, her voice changing with each character. Dallis's tone becoming full of emotion as the heroine wept with regret.

Dallis didn't realize that someone stood in the doorway listening.

"I think she fell asleep," Rory whispered.

Startled, Dallis dropped the book on the floor when her eyes met his. She'd sworn that it didn't matter if he ever came, but admitted now it was a lie. It mattered. Her heartbeat grew faster when he strode across the room to kneel at her feet. Rory lifted the book and put it in her lap, then stared into her eyes. Her eyes grew wider as he stayed close. Dallis felt the heat radiating off his body.

"You left," she said.

"No."

"I have a headache."

"Do you?" His eyes softened in concern, looking her over to see if she was indeed ill.

Dallis licked her lips and nodded to confirm she did. Her heart melted a little more toward him when he gently massaged her temples easing the pain away. His touch was soothing as he took care of her. All her anger disappeared. She needed him to stop. She raised her hand to brush his away, only to have him clutch it in his grasp and hold on. Rory brought her hand to his lips and placed a gentle kiss in her palm. Then, he laid her hand in her lap.

"I am sorry."

These three simple words, spoken with a deep emotion, settled in Dallis's soul. His troubled gaze searched hers for forgiveness. It was then Dallis saw the heavy burden he carried. She wondered of his troubles, but he was a proud man and wouldn't confide in her. If she forgave him, then what? Would he court her, or hide back in the shadows toying with her heart with every glance he devoured her with? Rory consumed her emotions. But would he reject her again? He waited before her, for an answer.

Dallis lifted her hand, her thumb caressing his face, easing his worries. A simple gesture accepting his apology. Rory closed his eyes at her gentle touch trying to wipe away his troubles. When he opened them to gaze into her eyes, he moved forward and pressed his lips against Dallis's. Whisper soft and then pulled away. Dallis sighed, and he wanted more, but held back. Then he decided, why not? When his lips began to move in to take her mouth in a more passionate kiss, he heard the footsteps of the butler outside in the hallway. He wasn't alone, another set echoed behind him. Rory stood quickly and walked over to the fireplace, putting a respectable distance between them.

Along the way he nudged Dallis's grandmother awake.

Chapter Eight

"Lady Dallis, Lord Holdenburg has arrived for afternoon tea."

"Thank you, Shaw."

Dallis stood and walked to greet Lord Holdenburg. "I did not think you would venture out in such horrible weather."

"It appears I am not the only one willing to risk a few drops of rain for your company."

"Yes, Lord Beckwith arrived but a few moments ago."

Dallis didn't elaborate on why Rory called. It was a private moment they shared. Hopefully one that would blossom into more. She noticed Rory's impatience, and how he kept glancing toward the door. Did he want to leave? Well, if that was the case Dallis wouldn't make it difficult for him. She didn't want him to remain if she was a burden to him. Rory had made his apology, and she'd accepted. While it meant a lot to her, obviously it didn't have the same impact on him. Dallis observed how the men acknowledged each other with nods, each regarding the other with narrowed eyes assessing the situation. Her grandmother was fully awake now, smiling mischievously at Dallis's predicament. Nanna took pleasure in the dominance radiating off the men filling the air with awkwardness for her.

"Beckwith."

"Holdenburg."

Holdenburg drew a deck of cards out of his suit pocket. "Lady Dallis, since we cannot take our daily walk, I thought we could play cards. I promised to teach you piquet."

"An excellent idea to pass the time on this dreary day. Will you join us, Lord Beckwith?" She offered him a clear option to remain or not.

"I do not play cards." Rory glared at Holdenburg, for the man knew the reason for his hatred of card games.

"Sorry, ol' chap, I forgot. Perhaps another time, Lady Dallis."

"You two play. Lord Beckwith shall keep me company," said Lady Ratcliff.

"Lord Beckwith?" Dallis asked him.

"Yes, Lady Dallis, and there is no better teacher in piquet than Lord Holdenburg here." Rory said, settling next to Lady Ratcliff on the sofa.

Lord Holdenburg moved a small table and rotated two chairs to sit across from one another near the fire, a distance away from them. Rory understood the man's intention. He was isolating Dallis from visiting with Rory while she learned the card game. This way Holdenburg could provide a more intimate atmosphere as their bond grew, while still in the company of others. He always was a sly one. Once a friend, now he stood as a threat.

Holdenburg settled Dallis into the chair, leaning over to say something in her ear before he sat across from her. A compliment to her dress whispered in a husky tone, he never would have spoken loud enough for her nanna to hear. Dallis felt the blush warming her cheeks, thankful for the fire so near to excuse her complexion if questioned. He was a naughty one. Dallis would need to keep her wits around him. She sensed Rory's eyes on her. Dallis turned her head to the side and realized he'd noticed her blush. Rory missed nothing. The intense way he regarded her caused Dallis to drop the cards Holdenburg dealt her. Why did Rory have the power to fluster her?

Holdenburg said, "Let me show you how to hold them. There is a trick to it."

Holdenburg scooped the cards into his hand, fanning them out. He then moved the cards, shifting them in a different order. Once he rearranged the cards, he tapped them together on the table, making them one. Then he slowly spread them out so only Dallis could see the numbers and suit. The cards now resembled a fan. Holdenburg lifted her hands and showed her how to hold the cards. He explained how she needed to keep them close to her body, and how to curve her hand to hide them from prying eyes. When Dallis tried to copy his actions, she drew laughter from him.

"No, more like this, Lady Dallis." Holdenburg's hands formed around hers, his fingers guiding her on how to hold the cards.

Dallis felt conflicted. His touch was firm yet gentle. From any other gentleman the directions would seem straightforward, yet with him they were a seduction. From his husky drawl to the attention of his hands when he instructed her. Yet, why did Lord Holdenburg not tempt her desires? The attention he'd displayed the last few days would have most ladies swooning, but Dallis merely felt comfortable. As if they were lifelong friends, not a gentleman courting her. She wouldn't lie, his attentions made her feel attractive. However, that was where they ended. The man who made her swoon sat behind her, not making any of the same efforts as Lord Holdenburg. Dallis wondered whether, if she displayed an interest in Holdenburg, Rory would react.

"You are a wonderful teacher, Lord Holdenburg," Dallis reached out to brush across his hand as he shuffled his cards.

Dallis's voice was low enough and her touch a gesture of affection to cause Rory to wonder if he was too late in his pursuit. He tightened his fingers into fists as Holdenburg seduced Dallis over a game of cards. Not only was he succeeding, Dallis seemed to take pleasure in Holdenburg's acts of seduction. From the blush gracing her cheeks to the touch of her hand. Their whispered words as they played cards portrayed a courtship moving swifter than he'd thought. Rory knew the game Holdenburg played on Dallis's affections, and the expected outcome. She would be heartbroken if Rory allowed this farce to continue. When he attempted to rise to interrupt their play, a hand stilled him. He looked at Lady Ratcliff, who shook her head, urging him to stay seated.

She said quietly, "No, you lost your right to interfere by your absence."

Rory also kept his voice low. The couple playing would hear but a murmur.

"I beg your pardon, Lady Ratcliff, but Lord Holdenburg is a scoundrel. I only wish to prevent Dallis from heartache."

Lady Ratcliff scoffed, "Little late for that, my boy,"

"She has already fallen for him?"

"I never figured you for a dense one."

"Another suitor?"

"The only gentlemen who call on Dallis now are scoundrels, rogues, and rakes. No thanks to you."

Rory cringed at her disgust. "Then who?"

"Were you hit too hard in the head on your last fight?"

"What do you know of my fighting?"

"Enough that you gain me extra pin money every week."

"How?" Rory scowled. He fought in the underbelly of London's seediest clubs. How did this sweet, old innocent lady have knowledge of his bouts?

"Don't you worry your thick skull on how I know things. Just start making right by Dallis or I will be a fight you will not win. Are we clear?"

"How can I, when she loves another?"

Lady Ratcliff shook her head and rolled her eyes at the heartsick man. She liked him. He would do her Dallis good. Dallis's parents had neglected their daughter and shipped her away somewhere at every opportunity. She needed a man like Rory Beckwith who would put her first above all others. The way he took care of his mother and sister were proof. He sacrificed much for them to keep their comfortable life, instead of the one they were dealt. At first, she suspected Rory to be a fortune hunter, like many poor men who held titles. However, as she watched him with his regard to Dallis, it was the complete opposite. It was why he stayed away. Which only endeared him in her eyes to be perfect for her granddaughter. After meeting his family, she decided he would be the one to make Dallis a bride.

"I guess you will have to discover a creative way to capture her heart. The question is, are you the gentleman for the challenge?"

Was he? After watching Holdenburg charm Dallis this afternoon, it set a pain in his gut. Rory could no longer stand by and see gentleman after gentleman try to win Dallis's heart. Her heart belonged to him and he no longer wanted to run away. An idea began to form. With a bit of help from his friends he would accept the challenge.

"I believe I am, Lady Ratcliff. If you will excuse me, I have a prior commitment I must attend. Please give my regards to Lady Dallis and tell her I found my visit most pleasurable." Rory rose and kissed Lady Ratcliff's hand with a wink before he left.

He never expressed his goodbye to Dallis or Lord Holdenburg. With a plan forming in his mind, Rory left the house. He would require Sidney and Sophia's help. Two of his friends who'd had experience in the matters of the heart lately. Rory would now listen to their advice.

Dallis saw him leave. He graciously kissed her nanna's hand before he left. Rory directed no words her way that he was taking his leave. His departure hurt. The game of flirting with Lord Holdenburg to make Rory jealous lost its enjoyment. When nanna released a cackle, Dallis swung to take notice of the glee on her grandmother's face. What brought Nanna happiness out of the blue? Dallis turned back to the game with Holdenburg, who sent her a quizzical glance, and she shrugged. She no longer took pleasure with the card game even though Lord Holdenburg was a patient teacher.

The dejected look upon Lady Dallis's face spoke volumes to Holdenburg. He realized it to be the fact of Beckwith's departure. He wasn't a simpleton to have not recognized her heart wanted another. While previously he was unsure of who held her affections, he now understood. Lady Dallis was in love with Beckwith and it was plain as day. But as usual his friend was mucking up a perfect opportunity.

Holdenburg was courting Lady Dallis as a "favor" to Lady Beckwith. She'd discovered some information regarding his past activities that he wished to be kept hidden for the time being. Lady Dallis was a lovely lady, but she wasn't the one for him. He began to understand Lady Beckwith's intentions. She wished to use him as a pawn to bring Rory to task. He chuckled to himself, deciding to take this courtship to a new level. The bloke deserved it for all the beatings and trouble they used to get into for their curiosity as lads. They scraped out of predicaments by the scruff of their necks many times, but through it all their friendship stood strong. Lately, that friendship had taken a turn for the worst. He only hoped he could repair it later after what he was about to do. He gathered the cards and slid them into the box.

"Thank you for entertaining me through this dreadfully rainy day, Lady Dallis. You have been a delight as always."

"Thank you, Lord Holdenburg, for teaching me how to play piquet."

"A complete pleasure. Now, I would like to extend an invitation for you and your grandmother to be my guests at the theater tomorrow evening. I also plan to invite Lady Beckwith and her daughter to join us."

"And Lord Beckwith?"

"Yes, of course. I wouldn't want to be the only gentleman surrounded by beautiful ladies. I can hear the gossip now."

Dallis laughed at the picture he described. "Your own personal harem."

"Yes. What every man desires."

"Do they?" Dallis asked innocently.

"Only the gentlemen who have not loved," he told her, looking deep into her eyes.

Flustered, Dallis glanced away.

"So, will your answer be yes? Shall I send a carriage around seven?"

Her grandmother answered for them. "We would love to go, young man." Her grandmother answered for them.

"Yes, it sounds delightful. I do enjoy the theater. Thank you for your kind offer."

"Excellent. I will be the envy of the ton with the most beautiful ladies in my box."

"Don't forget Lord Beckwith," Dallis reminded him.

"Yes, and Lord Beckwith."

Lord Holdenburg bid the ladies farewell and took his leave. He wanted to issue his invitation to Lady Beckwith in person. There were a few questions he needed answered before he continued with his pursuit of Lady

Dallis. While the pursuit of Lady Dallis would make Rory jealous enough to stake his claim, Holdenburg didn't want to ruin his chances with the one person who mattered the most. For years he'd patiently waited. When his courtship of Lady Dallis ended, Holdenburg would pursue the only lady he ever wanted but could never have.

Holdenburg would play the marker he won fair and square and let the cards fall where they may.

Chapter Nine

"Thank you for including me in your business venture." Rory rose and shook Sheffield's hand.

"With your knowledge of the financial market, you will be a great asset."

The two walked along the hall and discussed the procedure of the investment. They headed toward the parlor where Sophia had ordered them to join her for tea. When they entered the room, it was to find Sophia and Sidney sitting on the sofa with their heads bent together. They were probably plotting their next course of trouble. Not only were they whispering, but Wildeburg threw in a few comments of his own. Sheffield patted Rory on the shoulder as if in sympathy. Rory saw Sheffield shaking his head at the unspoken question, then turned back to the others, who had stopped their conversation once they were aware he entered the parlor.

"Rory, what a surprise," said Sophia.

"You invited me for tea," he reminded her.

"Yes, yes. Silly me."

Rory settled in a chair, watching the couples with suspicion as they sat around him, smiling like cats who caught the mouse. He was doomed. Rory had come here intending to ask for their advice, but now realized they had already decided his strategy to win Dallis's hand. Sidney and Sophia were two of his closest friends, and throughout the last few months since they had gotten married, the men in their lives accepted Rory into their circle of friendship. To be friends with these influential men of the ton meant doors now opened to him. His vote in Parliament, which in the past went unnoticed, now started having an impact. More men were listening to his viewpoints on bills.

"What?" he finally asked them.

"The kiss you gave Dallis ..." Sophia began.

"Was *soooo* romantic," Sidney said.

"However your behavior following ..." Wilde began.

"Has been atrocious," Sheffield growled to finish for them all.

Now the men sounded like their wives, finishing each other's sentences. Rory's head bounced back and forth between them as they berated his behavior. He was dizzy from the volley of insults directed at him. Each one of them pointing out his faults, one by one. He squirmed in his seat as they described his past actions. He held up his hands for them to cease. They all stopped in mid-sentence, waiting for him to speak.

"You are all correct. While I had business with Sheffield, I also wanted to seek your advice on how to win Dallis's hand. That is before Lord Holdenburg does."

"Lord Holdenburg is courting Dallis?" asked Sheffield.

"Yes. My mother introduced them."

Wilde whistled. "That is stiff competition, my friend. He is even more scandalous than I ever was."

"Lord *Holdenburg*," the ladies said in awe.

"Yes," Rory growled at their awe of the one man who stood in his way to Dallis's heart.

"So, what is your plan to court her?" Sidney turned serious now that they needed to establish a plan.

"I was hoping you could help me."

"Oh!" Sidney said, excited that somebody actually wanted her help in matchmaking.

Wilde and Sheffield shook their heads at Rory, mouthing to him the word *no*. He knew it was foolish to involve them, but he held no clue on how to repair the damage he'd done. Plus, these couples had found happiness from the hijinks of Sidney's devious mind. Why not him?

"I thought I would take her for a walk in the park. Perhaps feed the ducks like you enjoy, Phee."

"Rory, you cannot ever compare one lady to another while in the presence of said lady, even though you are only friends with the other said lady," Sidney explained.

"Why forever not?"

"No lady wants to hear of another while you are in pursuit of *her* hand. Even the demurest lady experiences jealousy."

"Did either of you?"

"Yes," both women stated.

"Try writing her letters," Sophia suggested, staring at Sheffield with a tender expression.

"Or have her visit a brothel in disguise." Wilde's joke was aimed toward Sheffield.

"Discover her favorite candy," said Sidney.

"Sneak into her room at night." Sheffield returned the poke toward Wilde.

All their suggestions came at once. The women leaned toward romance, while the men's ideas were more scandalous. More dangerous, but way more tempting. Turning his thoughts to the taste of her lips and the feel of Dallis in his arms, Rory was more led to the men's suggestions. The idea of Dallis in a brothel provoked wild images, but it wasn't a place he wanted to spend time with her. And the fear of her grandmother's cane would keep

Rory from Dallis's bedroom. Before he could even contemplate intimacy with Dallis, he needed to court her properly. Candy and letters? No, he needed to be more creative. Dallis wasn't a woman to be won over by trinkets. No, with her, his efforts must come from the heart.

"Thank you for your suggestions. While they might have worked on your own unorthodox courtships, I feel they would not for mine."

"Then what will you do?" asked Sidney.

"I shall take a more creative approach."

Sheffield said, "But you *will* take an approach? The lady deserves nothing less. Dallis is a friend of mine, and I will not have you keep destroying her good name because you are not man enough to claim her for yourself."

This angered Rory enough to rise and advance toward Sheffield. Business deal or not, the man held no right to defend Dallis. She was his responsibility. Twice now he'd watched this man almost destroy his friends, and Rory would not let Sheffield harm Dallis.

Wilde pulled Rory away from Sheffield. He knew Sheffield had only baited Rory to act. Instead Sheffield would end up beaten by the man again. Wilde sent Sidney a look asking to calm her friend. Sidney grabbed Rory's arm and led him toward the sofa to sit beside her. Wilde sent Sheffield a warning glare, only for the man to relax in his chair, wearing a smile of satisfaction.

"Rory, you must understand your actions, while they always have been gentlemanly, have turned into a scandalous rake. Dallis deserves better. All of us have your best interest at heart and we speak as your friends concerned for your reputation. Your behavior is not only causing you harm, think of your mother and sister."

Rory sighed and he finally admitted, "I am well aware of my actions and the consequences from them. However, poverty and not being able to provide for Dallis are what have kept me from courting her." He finally admitted.

"Which after today's deal will no longer be your excuse."

"That, and earlier today I had to watch Lord Holdenburg charm Lady Dallis. I wanted to punch the arrogant bastard."

The men laughed, having experienced the same feeling toward Rory.

"I could host another dinner party," Sidney suggested.

"NO!" Everybody shouted this at once, then laughed.

The last dinner party Sidney hosted, scandalous innuendoes were loudly spoken. There were tears, heartache, pleading, shocked guests, and new gossip for the ton. No, the last thing Rory needed was for Sidney to intervene on his part with another party.

He said, "While I appreciate your wonderful advice, I think I shall court Dallis in my own way."

"Good luck," the men muttered, while the women pouted on the sofa, because all their ideas for bringing Rory and Dallis together would not be allowed to hatch.

Talking to his friends about his problem eased Rory's doubts. However, he decided he would pursue Dallis on his own terms.

They needed their own love story.

Chapter Ten

When Rory returned home, he discovered Kathleen with her head pressed against the closed door to the parlor. He heard his mother talking softly with a man. Who was his mother visiting with? Did the debt collectors come calling when he was away? He needed to persuade his sister to stop her snooping so that he could take care of business. Rory knew that one day his mother would find out the complete mess his father left them in. He'd only hoped that it would have been later. Not now, while he tried to win Dallis's heart.

"I wonder what punishment Mother will bestow on you for your eavesdropping?"

"Shh," Kathleen whispered.

"I, myself, think that she should withhold Agnes's blueberry scones from you for a week."

Rory thought withholding Kathleen's favorite treat would entice her away. It was horrible enough that Mama would discover her husband's secrets. It was another thing for Kathleen to realize the depth of their father's depravity. Kathleen hero-worshipped their father, and Rory didn't want that memory to change.

"Rory, hush. I cannot hear what is being said with your annoying interference." She tried to wave him away.

"Kathleen, move away from the door this instance," Rory growled.

The only way for him to distract her attention was to display his displeasure. Rory would endure her anger in return for Kathleen not overhearing what was being discussed behind those closed doors. He grabbed her arm and started pulling her toward the staircase. Kathleen swatted at his hands and tried to wrench herself loose. When she dug in her heels and refused to move, Rory had no other choice. He lifted her up, threw her over his shoulder and started climbing the stairs. She thundered her fists on his back, calling him all sorts of names.

"I only wanted to listen to what that scoundrel wished to discuss with Mother. He strolled in all pompous and Mother gushed all over him like she always does. But I know the scoundrel has ulterior motives."

Rory stopped mid-step. Who did Kathleen refer to? His mother wouldn't gush over a shopkeeper. Whoever their mother entertained, it was somebody they were familiar with and set his sister on edge. Still, he needed to remove Kathleen so he could discover who the caller was for himself. However, before he could dispose of his sister, the parlor door opened. This was how their mother and guest found them. With Rory holding Kathleen upside-down, standing on the steps. His mother's astonished expression and the smirk of his former friend furthered Rory's frustration.

"Roderick Beckwith, put your sister down this instant!"

He narrowed his eyes at Holdenburg, lowering Kathleen to her feet. That only brought Holdenburg more pleasure. Rory saw his mother was deeply embarrassed at her children's hi-jinks. They had behaved as if they were young children instead of adults. Rory cringed at her disappointment. But the elegant lady only turned toward Lord Holdenburg and laughed.

"Children will be children, my lord. I am sorry for their behavior. If you would like to rescind your gracious offer, I would not lay fault."

"Their antics bring me delight, Lady Beckwith. I would still be honored if your family would be my guests at the theater tomorrow evening."

Kathleen gasped. Lord Holdenburg had invited them to watch a play. She loved the theater. When her eyes encountered his, Holdenburg tilted his head in the arrogant way she detested. What game did he play now? She wondered at why he would invite their family when Rory had not a thing to do with him since their father died.

"I promise they will be on their best behavior tomorrow evening. Thank you again for your generosity," Lady Beckwith replied.

"Excellent. I shall send word to Lady Ratcliff and Lady Dallis of your acceptance. Until tomorrow. Good day, my lady." Holdenburg kissed her mother's hand. "Beckwith." He nodded to Rory. "Lady Kathleen." He bowed before her with another smirk.

Kathleen humphed at his display and brushed her hair out of her eyes as she turned and climbed the staircase with as much dignity that she could muster. Considering that she only wore one slipper—the other had fallen off when her brother carried her like a sack of coal.

Holdenburg's invitation made perfect sense now. He wanted to taunt Rory with Dallis's affections. Kathleen would do everything in her power to keep them separated. But was she keeping Dallis and Holdenburg from each other for Rory's sake, or for her own?

~~~~~~

Rory watched Kathleen continue up the stairs. He closed his eyes at his foolishness. In the effort to protect her from learning the truth of their father's scandal, he'd embarrassed Kathleen in front of Holdenburg—of all people. He was aware of the crush Kathleen held for his old friend when she was younger, although she'd since outgrown the infatuation. Now Rory had humiliated her. He hoped Holdenburg wouldn't speak of this incident. Rory needed to find a way to gain Kathleen's forgiveness.

His mother's stare burned a hole in the back of his head. Rory sighed, turning toward her. He opened his mouth to speak only for her to hold her hand up.

She said, "I do not understand what has gotten into you lately. I am not even going to inquire why you had your sister tossed upside-down. However, I insist that you come to terms on whatever troubles you. As for tomorrow evening, you will accompany us and behave as the gentleman I have raised you to be." With that said she brushed past him on the stairs, making her way toward Kathleen's room.

Rory leaned on the railing as the weight of his mother's disappointment settled in his gut. Like the quick-tempered fool he was, he'd acted first before he understood the situation. He ran his fingers through his hair in frustration. But he wasn't only angry with himself. Holdenburg was the main cause. Holdenburg's invitation to join his party at the theater was to flaunt his courtship with Dallis. It wasn't only a message to Rory, but to the ton that he was an upstanding gentleman and not the scoundrel they painted him out to be. Rory knew better. He knew Holdenburg was a devious, conniving devil.

Rory started down the stairs and ran out of the house. Before Holdenburg could stake his claim on Dallis, Rory would warn him away.

He didn't have far to go. Holdenburg stood waiting outside of his carriage and talking with his driver. He pulled his watch out and noted the time.

"I expected you to storm out sooner," Holdenburg quipped.

"Whatever game you are playing, cease now."

"I play no game, friend."

"We are no longer friends. You lost that right with the hand you played."

"One day you will understand why I played that hand."

"I highly doubt it. Leave her alone."

"Which *her* are we referring to?"

"Dallis," Rory growled.

"Oh, the lovely Lady MacPherson. Now, why would I leave her alone? Have you spoken for her?"

Rory didn't answer. He couldn't, and Holdenburg knew it.

"Right, then. Until tomorrow evening, Beckwith."

Holdenburg climbed into his carriage. Rory clenched his fists as his competition drove away. While he wanted nothing more than to punch the conceit off Holdenburg's face, he wished to avoid his mother's wrath over his temper.

Chapter Eleven

Kathleen waited in the foyer for her mother to join them. She kept her contempt toward Lord Holdenburg silent, pretending pleasure at his invitation to the theater. The only reason she joined the party was because of her love for the theater. She enjoyed the actors as they delved into their characters and brought the stories to life. Kathleen loved to escape into the drama as if she was part of the performance. The play was a comedy that she had never seen before and held rave reviews.

Throughout his friendship with Rory, Lord Holdenburg always ignored Kathleen as if she were a pest. She'd resented him whenever he took Rory away on adventures and left her behind. As she grew older, Kathleen watched him charm every woman of the ton, either into his bed or have them cater to his every whim. Even her own mother thought him a dear and always spoiled him as a son when he visited.

Even now, he infuriated Kathleen with his casual indifference. Holdenburg paid no compliment to her dress, and he held no pleasure in her company to this evening's festivities. She at least thought he would admire the new ribbon she wove through her hair.

Rory had left it on her pillow that afternoon. It was his way of apologizing for his boorish behavior yesterday. She still didn't understand why he tried to remove her from outside the parlor door. All she tried to do was find out what Holdenburg and her mother discussed. When he had arrived, Holdenburg asked to speak to her mother alone. Her mother sent

Kathleen off to help Agnes with dinner. Instead, Kathleen stood outside the door to listen for any clue to why he called. Because of Rory's outlandish behavior, she never found out why. Kathleen never stayed mad at her brother for any length of time. So she accepted his apology and wore the new ribbon.

However, Holdenburg stared at her in an ungentlemanly fashion as they waited. He leaned against the wall with his feet crossed in a casual manner, patiently waiting for her mother.

Lord Holdenburg was dressed to perfection. From his top hat to the tails of his evening jacket. Not one bit of lint or wrinkle graced his clothing. No man should appear so sinfully delicious. From his dark, black hair, to his sensuous eyes, to the fine fit of his clothes, he was the perfect specimen. Even the devil-may-care attitude he flung around enticed men and women to his *persona*. But not her. She recognized the devil himself disguised in his form. She wanted to strike out against his smugness.

"Mama is only using you to make Rory jealous of your attention to Lady Dallis."

Lord Holdenburg pushed himself off the wall and strolled toward Kathleen. His steps were lazy and slow as they took him to stand before her. He stroked his finger along her cheek and leaned over to whisper in her ear.

"I am well aware of your mother's plans, for they fit in perfectly with mine."

His soft words and touch sparked a reaction Kathleen never felt before. In her confusion, Kathleen reached a hand to her cheek and gazed into his eyes. His expression changed swiftly before Kathleen understood his intent. Now only amusement lit his blue eyes as he greeted her mother. Her confusing thoughts regarding Lord Holdenburg kept Kathleen from joining the conversation as they rode toward Lady Ratcliff's home where

they gathered Lady Dallis and her grandmother. Rory would meet them at the theater.

Kathleen's eyes kept straying toward Holdenburg throughout their ride. Once, while she conversed with Dallis, he directed a look in her direction that led Kathleen's thoughts in a direction unknown. When she glanced back at him, it was to find his attention fixed on Dallis. Kathleen was mistaken, Holdenburg only had eyes for Dallis.

Dallis was saying, "My Lord, it appears your wish for a harem has come true."

"You are mistaken, Lady Dallis, I said most men would wish for this, not I."

"Wish for a what?" Kathleen inquired.

"Lord Beckwith will join our party at the theater." Holdenburg interrupted before Dallis answered Kathleen.

Dallis met his gaze and realized that Holdenburg didn't want Kathleen to have knowledge of their previous conversation. She sent him a swift nod of understanding. To change the subject and draw Kathleen's attention away, Dallis discussed the play they were about to attend.

~~~~~

Rory impatiently waited for them to arrive. The box was luxurious with every chair draped in comfortable cushions. Holdenburg even had his own servant waiting to serve champagne. He even supplied each woman with a new fan to cool themselves in the overcrowded theater. Every comfort to make the evening enjoyable were within their grasp. This display would threaten most men, but Rory knew it only to be in Holdenburg's nature. His old friend was a charming soul who liked to please. Rory couldn't feel threatened by him even if he tried.

When the box became invaded by Holdenburg's party, Rory rose to his feet and guided his mother to her seat as the earl helped Lady Ratcliff to hers. Once the gentlemen settled the two older ladies, Rory was turning to assist Dallis when an elbow nudged his side. With a glare, Rory elbowed back and reached Dallis first, guiding her to a seat toward the back of the balcony hidden in the shadows. Rory sat next to her, sending Holdenburg a victorious look. Holdenburg returned it with a glare and then offered to escort Kathleen to her seat. Kathleen sent Rory her own scowl of displeasure before she settled at the front of the balcony.

The theater was a treat Rory had been unable to gift Kathleen with since their father passed away. Rory always enjoyed Kathleen's pleasure as she became engrossed in the performances. Holdenburg was gracious to provide them with this gift. Rory chuckled as Holdenburg took the only remaining seat in the box, next to his sister, and watched as Holdenburg attempted to talk to his sister only for Kathleen to rebuke him. Seeing Holdenburg rebuffed by his sister might be more entertaining than the play itself. Before Rory took pleasure from that, he should probably see what he accomplished for himself with Dallis.

"You are exquisite this evening, Lady Dallis."

And she was with her hair in a riot of curls and a dress of soft blue encased around her generous curves. Dallis's creamy skin glowed under the candlelight. Rory wished he could reach out to trace his fingers across the soft surface.

"You're very gracious, Lord Beckwith."

"I only speak the truth from my eyes as I gaze upon your beauty."

Dallis blushed at his compliment. She saw how he fought with Lord Holdenburg to escort her to their seats. He'd settled them in the darkest corner. Was this another attempt to seduce her and not respond? It would only cause the scandal surrounding her name to grow. She hoped not. Dallis wished his attempt to visit her yesterday meant that Rory would court her properly. She was beginning to doubt everybody's opinions on his regard.

The theater became engulfed in darkness. The stage lit up with the characters coming to life. The scenes in the backdrop, drawing the eye to the fine detail, enhanced the performance. Dallis attempted to watch the play, but the couple in front drew her attention. The play plainly captivated Kathleen, her lips moved along with the characters as if she was the actress herself. However, that wasn't what drew her eye, but Lord Holdenburg. He regarded Rory's sister with devotion. Did he care for Kathleen? And they weren't the only distraction. With Rory sitting so close, Dallis found it difficult to concentrate on the witty banter on the stage. Rory's eyes were focused on her.

Rory tried to hold back, but he needed to touch her. Dallis's hands rested in her lap, holding onto the fan. He put his hand on hers, causing Dallis to drop the fan on the floor. It went unnoticed. Rory peeled the gloves from both his hands and Dallis's, and intertwined their fingers. When she raised her eyes to his, he smiled and turned his attention to the stage.

Dallis relaxed when Rory simply held her hand as they enjoyed the performance. His smile softened her guard as she took comfort from his touch. Rory's hand was rough from hard callouses against the softness of her own. Before she was aware of her intent, she explored the differences. Her fingers trailed across the scrapes in his knuckles, and Dallis wondered why his hands were beaten. When she touched an open sore, his grip tightened. Dallis stroked the area gently and he relaxed.

Rory stilled at her touch. He only meant to hold her hand in an act of his true intentions. But with the gentle exploration of her touch his thoughts took a turn toward pleasure. How would she respond if he acted out his true desires? Would she sigh in pleasure? He took notice of how far they were hidden in the darkness. They were safe from any prying eyes. He stroked his thumb across her wrist where the beat of her pulse quickened. With his other hand he traced the length of her neck, low across her chest. Rory heard Dallis's sharp intake of breath, but she didn't halt his actions. If anything he sensed a need for more. He lowered his head to follow the path of his fingers with his tongue. His lips started right below her ear, kissing softly before his tongue slid down. She tasted like strawberries. Her sigh echoed in his ears as he licked across the neckline of her dress.

Dallis's body was melting into her seat as Rory attacked her senses with his sensuous mouth. His highly scandalous behavior would be the final straw to her ruination if they were caught. When his hands brushed across her breasts and his thumb teased her nipples, Dallis was past the point of caring anymore. Rory could ruin her twenty times over as long as did not cease his touch. When her sigh turned into a moan that others could hear, he captured her mouth in a mind-numbing kiss. His lips drawing out each of her desires into a kiss filled with passion. Rory's hand slid inside to caresses her breasts, and Dallis's moans turned to groans that made his kiss even more powerful. With each stroke of his tongue he demanded more passion. Dallis's fingers slid into his hair, arching her body closer to him.

Her damn chair was in the way. When Dallis pressed closer to him, Rory almost came undone. With a growl, he swept her onto his lap and wrapped Dallis in an embrace. In the back of his mind he understood the danger of their entanglement, but was past caring. Rory needed her. The weeks of trying to avoid Dallis wore on his patience. Her kisses met his demands with promises of more. Each breath from her into him, increased his appetite. Rory only meant for one taste, but his body wasn't satisfied, it only wanted more. He pulled his fingers from her breasts and slid them along her leg. Rory's hand moved higher, teasing her thighs to open for him.

When his thumb brushed across her wetness, he moaned into her kiss capturing her sighs of pleasure. His fingers sunk into her heated core, melting Dallis against him.

Oh my, was all Dallis thought of to say. How wonderfully, delightfully, scandalous. The pleasures he taught her body only made her wish for more. Rory's touch sent her emotions floating on a sensation out of her control. Each strum of his finger inside her wetness caused an ache needing to be relieved. Her body responded, begging for him to continue. Dallis wanted to stroke the hardness of his chest with her hand. When her fingers tried to unbutton his shirt, he stilled. Rory dropped his head to Dallis's forehead, taking deep breaths. He removed his hand from under her dress and brought both of her hands to his lips for a kiss. Rory's stared into Dallis's eyes, revealing his struggle. He righted her clothing, then slid her off his lap and onto her chair. After she settled, Rory slid her gloves back onto her hands. With a final brush of his thumb across her lips, he slid on his own gloves and resumed his attention to the play as if nothing untoward had happened. However, something did. Dallis noticed the pulse beating in his neck rapidly, as did her heart for him.

Soon candles were lit and applause erupted around them. Dallis understood why he put a halt to his affections. Intermission began with the crew preparing for Act II. Rory leaned over and gathered the fan from the floor, opened it and placed it in her hand.

"You may want to cool yourself, my dear, before people realize my intentions."

Dallis flicked the fan back and forth to freshen her heated body. "And what are your intentions, Lord Beckwith?"

"You will discover soon enough, Lady Dallis," he replied, helping her to rise.

Kathleen rushed toward them, exclaiming her delight on the wonderful performance. She described the set and the costumes as if they hadn't watched the show—which was the truth. Rory was too busy enjoying the pleasures of Dallis. A becoming shade of pink graced Dallis's cheeks. Dallis indulged his sister with questions, asking her opinion of the performance. She made Kathleen feel as if she was more knowledgeable, a kindness which only endeared Dallis to him even more. His sister meant the world to him and Rory indulged her more than he ought. Ever since the day Kathleen was born and his mother laid her in Rory's arms, he'd sworn to protect her from all that was harmful. To this day Kathleen was still unaware of the true nature of their father's demise. Something that Rory hoped she would never discover, for it would destroy her love of life. No, Rory would continue to protect Kathleen for as long as he could.

Dallis's mind was in a whirl. Rory's sister was a delight. Kathleen's love of the theater was captivating as she retold the play. Which in Dallis's case was a blessing. For throughout the first act, a certain gentleman and the power of his touch occupied all her attention. Dallis still blushed from what they'd done. It didn't help how close Rory stood by her side now, almost protectively. Dallis tried listening to Kathleen's descriptions, but her mind kept wandering to his promise. What will she discover soon enough? These thoughts vanished when Lord Holdenburg joined them. Then she only felt remorse. Dallis had let Rory dominate her time when she should have spent more with Lord Holdenburg who'd invited them here this evening. As much as she wished to continue the evening with Rory, her guilty conscience guided her to the earl.

"Lord Holdenburg, what a joy this evening has been so far. Thank you for this wonderful treat."

"You are very welcome, Lady Dallis. It is always a pleasure to spoil a beauty such as yourself."

"Humph," Kathleen muttered low enough, but all still heard it.

Lord Holdenburg directed a glare in her direction. Rory pulled Kathleen away toward their mother and Dallis watched them in confusion. She didn't understand Kathleen's attitude toward Lord Holdenburg. Dallis continued to stare as Rory poured her grandmother and his mother a glass of champagne while lecturing his sister. Kathleen pouted and stomped over to her chair, picking up her theater glasses to observe the changing of the stage. Rory inquired to his mother's comfort before he took the seat next to Kathleen. He wrapped his arms around her shoulders and whispered to her. Soon Rory had Kathleen smiling and she rewarded him with a kiss on the cheek. Another part of Dallis's wall broke toward him. The orchestra played a few notes warning the attendants the second act was about to begin.

Holdenburg told Dallis, "It appears you have lost your escort, shall we take our seats?"

"I apologize for Lord Beckwith's rude behavior earlier."

"Never fear, my lady. We have been competing since we were old enough to understand. Any man would feel threatened if they were striving to win your hand. Rory might have started the play with you, however, I am the one you will end the performance with. Therefore, I win the chance of remaining in your memory the longest. Every gambler knows when to play his hand. It is not my fault Rory played his too soon."

"I am a card game then?"

"No, my dear, you are the prize."

Dallis wasn't sure if she should be furious. Card game? Prize? Was how she wished for Rory to pursue her any different? She had taken the advice of Sidney and Sophia to make Rory jealous with another man. Should Dallis be angry with Lord Holdenburg when ultimately she was the one using him? Frankly, it wasn't in her character to behave in this manner. After this evening, the next time Lord Holdenburg requested a walk, she would confide and set him free. If she wanted to win Rory's heart, she would do it in her own way. With her own weapons of love. And in the end, if Rory didn't respond, then he wasn't the man for her.

Dallis tried to concentrate on the second half of the play, but her gaze kept straying to Rory. He sat relaxed in his chair, laughing with his sister at the antics of the actors. She wished for him to continue what he started. Dallis shut out her thoughts of Rory and tried to entice Lord Holdenburg into a conversation. However, the gentleman was distracted in his own right and payed no attention toward her. His fingers drummed silently on the arm of the chair, his gaze focusing forward. Even though they were in the darkest part of the box, Dallis saw the depth of sadness reflected in his eyes. They held a look of longing that she related to only so well. He was watching Lady Kathleen. Dallis wasn't mistaken—Lord Holdenburg cared for Lady Kathleen.

"You care for her?" Dallis whispered.

"Who, Lady Dallis?" His voice turned cold and restrained.

"Lady Kathleen."

Lord Holdenburg's cynical laughter confused Dallis. "For Lady Kathleen? No, my lady, it is you who I care for, not for some overindulged debutante."

He lifted her hand to place a kiss against her gloved fingers. The kiss held no distraction, for his denial was too strong. Also, his kiss left her empty. It reminded Dallis too much of Rory's intimacies from before. Dallis felt guilty for allowing Holdenburg to touch her, let alone kiss her. She tried pulling her hand from his grasp, but he held on smiling indulgently.

That was how the ton remembered their affections, when the theater lit at the end of the play. Even Rory and his sister displayed their displeasure. Dallis noticed Rory's anger and the hurt expression on Kathleen's face. She longed to shout at them they were wrong, but couldn't.

"Smile, Lady Dallis, or the ton will think you play loose with your favors. I would hate for your name to endure any more scandal."

Dallis smiled at Lord Holdenburg so as not to draw any more attention to embarrass Nanna. Lord Holdenburg's behavior shocked her. Since their introduction, he'd portrayed a fun-loving bachelor who enjoyed courting her. The man holding her hand spoke of a dangerous chap who could ruin her in a moment's notice. His quick change of behavior at the mere mention of a slip of a girl, only confirmed in Dallis's mind where his affections lay. If Holdenburg thought he could threaten Dallis, then she would play along long enough to gather any information she needed. Men like Lord Holdenburg never scared Dallis before and wouldn't now.

"Think twice, Lord Holdenburg, to frighten me. Now I know your weakness." Dallis said with a glance at Kathleen, wrenching her hand away.

The Beckwiths offered their gratitude before Rory escorted his mother and sister home. The carriage remained quiet with her grandmother resting in the corner. Holdenburg and Dallis regarded each other. Neither one of them smiling. They each pondered how much to trust the other with their secrets, and how they could help one another.

"A walk in the park tomorrow?" he suggested.

"Yes, a walk in the park tomorrow."

Chapter Twelve

As Dallis assisted her nanna to her room and into bed, she realized nerves would prevent any sleep of her own. Her nanna had given the servants the evening off. She spoiled the devoted staff with her carefree whims. This evening was one of those times. Dallis decided a cup of warm milk while reading before the fire would help make her sleepy. After making the milk, she wandered into the library looking for a new book to read. This evening had ended different from had been expected with a mystery to everybody's feelings. Unsure of her interest, Dallis trailed her fingers across the tomes searching for the right book.

"What is your desire, my dear?"

Dallis turned in fright, one hand to her chest. She searched in the darkness to discover Rory lounging in a chair near the fireplace. He'd discarded his suit jacket, unbuttoned his vest, and tossed his cravat over the arm of the chair.

Dallis's voice caught in her throat, devouring him with her eyes.

"Dallis, do you wish to read a mystery?"

She shook her head.

"A book about flowers?"

Another shake of her head.

"Yes, too boring. How about history?

She gulped and still couldn't speak.

"Mmm, perhaps a romantic novel?"

By this time he'd stood and come next to her, gliding his fingers over the books, until his hand rested next to hers. He kissed her fingers one by one.

"Why read about it when you can live it?"

Before she replied, he gathered Dallis in his embrace and kissed her passionately. His lips coaxed hers to open to savor her sweetness. They were warm and made him hungry for more. Rory knew he was the devil for breaking into her house. Well, he didn't actually *break* in. Lady Ratcliff's servants needed to learn to lock the windows. Still, he shouldn't be here, but their time this evening whetted his appetite to see her. When Rory watched Holdenburg force his act of dominance on Dallis at the end of the play, it took every ounce of Rory's control to keep his anger contained. Now that they were alone, he would finish what he started.

Rory lifted Dallis and carried her over to the chair, resting her on his lap. He pulled away from the sweet temptation of her lips to gaze at Dallis in the candlelight. Unbound hair hung to her waist, the redness blazing brighter against the firelight, darkening the blonde. The sheer, virginal nightgown displayed her charms. Dallis's womanly curves enticed him to peel the garment from her body to view for his own pleasure. However, he resisted the temptation. As much he wanted to act out his desires, Rory wouldn't risk her grandmother finding them together. But it didn't mean he couldn't play for a bit. Just a few more kisses to satisfy him until she became his.

Dallis knew she should be asking how he gained access inside the house. And also rebuff his advances. Instead she glorified at the wonderful sensation of being held in Rory's arms. His kisses and touch drugged her senses with pleasure. She only desired more. This evening his attentions only gave her a craving of what she missed. Dallis would be more than a willing participant if he showed her. Along the way, maybe she could capture his heart.

Her hands settled on his chest. Rory's warmth seeped through his clothing. Dallis moved her fingers, caressing his chest through the shirt's opening. Rory's body tensed as she pressed his smooth flesh. She slipped the studs from his shirt, opening it wider, needing to touch him as he touched her earlier. Her hands spread his shirt apart, and Dallis trailed her fingers down to his stomach. At his groan of pleasure, Dallis was aware of her power over him. She raised her eyes and watched his eyes darkening to a field of the darkest green. She lowered her head and placed a kiss on his collarbone, then worked her way along his neck. Reaching his ear, his breath quickened. The hands on her hips tightened as Dallis brushed her breasts against Rory's chest.

She was madness. He came here to seduce her, and she ended up being the one to seduce him. Her touch set him on fire. His cock hardened as her soft bottom pressed into him. How could Rory resist her sweetness? Dallis's body ached for his touch. If he started, he didn't know if he could stop, but yet his need was stronger than his control. He lost all of it when she whispered in his ear.

"I thought I might live it, instead of reading about it. Mmm, seems to me I am the only one living it. Did you want to read about it, Rory?"

"Do not tease me, Dallis."

She traced her tongue across his bottom lip. "Who is teasing whom, Rory?"

Her tongue kept tracing his lips until he opened them. Dallis took the claim on the kiss, exploring his mouth like he usually did to her. Rory held back, letting her play. When her tongue slid across his, he responded. When she slid his bottom lips between hers and gently sucked, he groaned into her kiss. After his groan, her kiss changed. She was no longer playful, but demanding. The stroke of her tongue became stronger, urging him to release his passion. Rory answered Dallis's wish by taking possession of her mouth. Their kiss taking control of their emotions. She wrapped her arms around his neck, clinging tight.

Dallis trembled, their passion turning into a need stronger than anything he could handle. Her body melted around him. Rory rose and lowered her before the fire. As he laid next to her, he gazed into her eyes. They spoke of her need for him. He wanted her so much he couldn't control it, if he took her.

"Dallis."

"Rory, please kiss me."

"Oh dear, I want to do more than kiss you."

Dallis reached for his hand. She saw the hesitation in his eyes and realized his honor prevented him from becoming more intimate. This moment, like all the others, he fought against dishonoring her. While he still tasted her he kept a tight rein on his control. Dallis only wanted him to break free to show his true intentions. She decided to take the lead, like in the novels Sophia loaned her. They differed from the ones she read to her grandmother. The stories were scandalous, and they taught a few things she wanted to try. Dallis unbuttoned her nightdress and guided his hand to her breasts. When his hand settled on her chest, he closed his eyes as his thumb brushed across her nipple, and she moaned. When Rory opened his eyes again, he saw her reaction and caressed her nipples into hardened pebbles.

Once he realized she wanted more than his touch, he lowered his head and slid a nipple into his mouth. Dallis moaned louder, and the pleasure shot through her body when his tongue slid back and forth across teasing them. She ran her fingers through his hair, holding him to her breasts. What she read about didn't compare to the reality. Rory held her breasts and loved them as if they were precious gems.

Dallis tasted more exquisite than Rory could ever imagine. He needed to put a stop to this madness before he took her on the hard floor. When she guided him to her breasts, he couldn't resist the sweet treat. She tasted like strawberries. As he drew the sweet buds into his mouth, the flavor of berries exploded under his tongue. Rory wanted one touch. He slid his hand under her gown, sinking into her wetness, drawing a tight bud into his mouth. Dallis's body arched into him as he stroked her.

"Rory, Rory," she moaned.

The sound of his name on her lips sunk deep into his soul. Rory needed to stop before he was beyond control. When Dallis moaned his name again, it would be in his bed where he would make love to her all night. Not ruin her and force Dallis into a marriage she may not want. No, he wanted to win her heart the old-fashioned way. For him to achieve that, he must pull away from their passion. No matter how pleasurable it was and how his body protested the need to make Dallis his. *One more touch*, he promised as his finger continued to stroke her, but one was not enough. Rory's body overruled his mind as he continued to pleasure her. He watched the desire in Dallis's eyes as he brought her pleasure to new heights. Dallis was a temptress he didn't want to resist. From her passionate eyes to her responsive body held in his arms.

The touch of his fingers drove Dallis insane. With each stroke she fell deeper in love with him. While some would describe this emotion as lust, it was far from what she felt. Lust only lasted for a brief moment in time. Love created memories that you craved to last a lifetime. This was love. She craved Rory with a love that had no explanation. His touch, his kisses, and his gaze reached a part of her soul only meant for him. Dallis wanted Rory to make her his with a desperate need, but recognized the self-control in his eyes. She wanted him to lose the control, but understood his reason to resist. Dallis should feel shameless, spread out in front of the fire, guiding him to explore her body, instead she felt free. Free from the stipulations placed on her by society. Free from the expectations her parents placed upon her to marry well. Free from herself.

She traced her thumbs under his eyes to release the pressures of life from his gaze. Rory carried heavy burdens, and Dallis didn't want to become another burden to him. A wrong he would insist to make a right, if they continued. If he wanted to court her properly, then she would wait for him. She guided his lips to hers where she placed a kiss that relayed her understanding of the demons he fought. Rory pulled his hands away and wrapped her tight, kissing her back. Soft. Sweet. Gentle.

Rory rolled over and brought Dallis across his body. Her hair splayed across his chest, and he let his fingers stroke the long strands. Her hair was soft against him. He brought a lock to his nose and inhaled the sweet scent of strawberries.

"You smell like a strawberry."

Dallis laughed. "That is because I mix them in my soap."

"Mmm, I thought maybe you were a giant strawberry, meant for me to devour."

Dallis swatted him. "Giant, huh?"

Rory ran his palms across her body, enjoying her curves. "No, sorry love, just the right size to bite." He bit at her neck.

Dallis giggled. The natural sensation of lying in his arms confirmed they were made for each other. She quieted from his teasing to enjoy the pleasure of his caresses. Dallis yawned, feeling her body drifting to sleep. She fought to keep her eyes open, not wanting to lose what time they had alone. However, her last few sleepless nights took its toll.

Rory knew the moment she drifted away in slumber. Her body became soft and relaxed curving into his body. Her giggles ceased and her breathing deepened. He continued to touch her, gentle against her soft skin. Dallis's moans in her sleep kept him from rising. Each moan urged him to continue. If he made her sleep pleasurable, it warmed his heart. However, before long he would need to rise and carry Dallis to her bedroom.

Along the way he hoped he didn't encounter her grandmother.

Chapter Thirteen

When Dallis awoke the next morning she lay tucked under the covers with her nightgown rebuttoned. Rory must have carried her to bed. The last thing she remembered was feeling secure in his arms as she fell asleep. Dallis closed her eyes, remembering their time in the library. A warm blush spread over her body as the scandalous thoughts flooded her senses. The emotions he drew with his kisses and touch made Dallis wish to experience more. She rose swiftly and dressed for the day. She wanted to be available for Rory when he called. Because she knew today he wouldn't disappoint her. He wouldn't have been as intimate, if he didn't mean to court her.

As she walked closer to the parlor, she overheard her grandmother talking with a man. Dallis hurried, believing it to be Rory. His presence this early meant only one thing. It warmed her heart that he wished to see her as much as she wished to see him.

Instead disappointment filled her heart when she found her grandmother entertaining Lord Holdenburg. He was the last man she wanted to visit with, even though she promised him a walk in the park. Perhaps she could persuade him to stay indoors, then she wouldn't miss the chance of Rory's visit.

"There you are, lass. I was explaining to Lord Holdenburg how unusual it was for you to lie in bed so late."

"I am sorry for the lateness of my rising. I found it difficult to fall asleep, so I thought if I read it would make me tired."

"Yes. Shaw found your full glass of milk this morning."

"Another reason to apologize. I am sorry, Nanna, the story absorbed my attention."

Holdenburg said, "I like to pass the time with a great novel myself. May I inquire to the title of the book?"

Dallis's mind scrambled to think of a title. Of the hundreds of novels she read, she couldn't recall a single one. All she remembered was the trail of kisses Rory spread across her chest when he lowered her to the floor and loved her. She tried to focus on the new dilemma but all she could do was shrug her shoulders in forgetfulness.

"I am sorry, I forgot the title. After I finished reading, I slid the book back onto the shelf."

He smiled. "No problem, perhaps on our walk you can explain the plot and I can try to place the story."

"Yes, our walk. Perhaps instead you can continue to teach me how to play cards? I think I have a knack for card games."

"I confess, Lady Dallis, I hoped we could take a stroll through the park. It has been miserable being stuck indoors through the latest rainfall. I promise on my next visit, I can teach you more."

"Go for a walk, Dallis. You look pale this morning. A walk will brighten your cheeks with some sun. Only do not forget your bonnet. Your mother will have my head if you get any more freckles."

Dallis blushed. "Yes, Nanna."

~~~~~

"I admire your delightful freckles," Lord Holdenburg murmured as they strolled along the pathway in the park.

Dallis blushed and decided not to comment on his compliment. She was in no mood to flirt with Holdenburg after his behavior the evening before. To encourage him would only cause difficulties later with Rory. She discovered through Kathleen that Rory and Holdenburg were lifelong friends who always had healthy competitions on everything. Kathleen explained that lately her brother had distanced himself from Holdenburg due to family obligations, but Dallis wondered if this wasn't for other reasons. She didn't want to pit the two gentlemen against each other for her affections. There was only one she desired to gift her affections to, and that man was Rory. After the glances she'd witnessed Lord Holdenburg direct toward Kathleen, she had no doubt where his affections lay.

Their walk ended near the Serpentine. Even though the rain stopped, it didn't take away the gusts of wind. The day was warmer, but the breeze still sent the water into white caps, causing the boats secured to the docks to bash against each other. Dallis watched the destruction, waiting for Lord Holdenburg to explain himself. However, he stayed silent. When she glanced his way, she noticed him staring across the river toward a couple chasing after a girl's bonnet. It wasn't any girl, but Kathleen. Her companion grabbed the ribbons and rescued the hat before it floated away in the water. Dallis watched the delight that spread across Kathleen's face, then turned to observe Lord Holdenburg's reaction. He frowned before, trudging back up the hill to settle on a bench. The look of disappointment on his face relieved any anger she felt toward the lord.

She said, "So, I was correct in my assumption?"

"Yes."

"Then why have you entered into a courtship with me? Why do you not court Lady Kathleen?"

"It is a long story, Dallis."

She laughed. "I love long stories." She nudged him with her shoulder.

He barked out a laugh. "Well, for starters, she despises me."

"Nonsense."

"You saw for yourself how she reacts toward me."

"Then change her mind."

"Oh, if it were only that simple, my dear."

"Everything is simple, if you want it badly enough."

"How is that going for you? Have you recently brought Rory to heel?"

"Yes, I believe so."

"Mmm …"

Dallis frowned. "You do not believe he has stopped letting his responsibilities stand in his way?"

"It is more than responsibilities, Dallis dear."

"How so?"

"It is a manner of pride."

"I do not understand."

"Dallis, it is not my place to explain to you Rory's private affairs. Rory must explain his problems to you. However, I can say, he would not be the only man to suffer from pride if they wanted to make you their bride."

"We are a sorry lot are we not, Lord Holdenburg?"

"Yes, I believe we are."

"You want the sister and I want the brother. But yet here we are together."

"We could not be any worse off. Perhaps we ought to set our feelings to the side regarding them and focus on each other?"

"You know as well as I, we would only grow to resent one another."

Lord Holdenburg sighed. "Correct as usual. Then what do you suggest?"

"I suggest we pursue the ones we most desire until we reach the outcome meant for us."

"For me to achieve that, I must sink to the lowest depths of a scoundrel."

"Lowest depths, huh? I never figured your character to be dramatic, but considering where your heart lies it could work out perfectly. Lady Kathleen is drawn to the theater. You could be the dastardly villain who the heroine tames into the hero of her dreams."

They each fell into a fit of laughter at the vivid description of his behavior he needed to portray.

"And you, Dallis, how will you bring Rory around?"

"I already have. In fact, I would not be surprised if he is waiting for me at Nanna's right this instance."

"Then by all means, let us return you to his regard."

Dallis laughed again when Lord Holdenburg tugged her to her feet and they returned to her grandparent's townhome.

"I hope you can forgive my behavior from the previous evening."

"You are forgiven. Please, do not be a stranger, Lord Holdenburg. I wish to aide you in your dilemma whenever you have the need."

He bowed and lifted her hand for a kiss. "Thank you, my lady. Now hurry, your prince awaits your arrival.

But he didn't. Nor did he arrive at all throughout the day. Dallis waited in anticipation for Rory with every knock on the door. After every countless visitor Shaw announced, her heart broke a little more. As usual, Rory betrayed her confidence in him. When she readied for bed, Dallis continued to wait for any sign: a letter, a gift, or a word from his mother or sister. But nothing. Dallis wiped the tears trailing along her cheeks as the hurt returned. Why? Why did he give her hope and then snatch it away?

~~~~~~~

Rory slumped in the chair behind his desk. He lifted the glass and drank the spirits in one swallow. Still it didn't numb the feeling in his gut. After a couple of more drinks, he began to see the light behind his troubles. They'd started near dawn and only just ended. He handled them all but one. The one that tore at his gut all day because he never got to call on Dallis. He'd failed her once more. Every time he settled a crisis and meant to sneak away for a few minutes to Dallis, another problem would blow up in his face. Damn his father for still causing them trouble from the grave.

Rory knew that by not calling on Dallis today or sending word, he hurt her deeply. His gesture tomorrow would have to be so grand for any hope of forgiveness. All day, he thought of her sweet nature as he held her while she slept. Rory had a special gift that he would hand over personally. He wanted to give Dallis the best of everything, but because of his late father he couldn't. The simple gesture would bring her delight, and the treasure only cost his family from enjoying a special treat. Rory had convinced cook to let him have the strawberries she wanted to make into a jam. Agnes thought him peculiar when he put them in a jar with a simple cover. He wrote a note and attached it to the jar. The gift rested on his desk waiting to be delivered. A job he would see to himself in the morning. Rory decided no further interruptions would prevent him from capturing Dallis's smile and holding it close.

He moved the chair closer to the desk, pouring over the ledgers one more time. His glance kept straying to the jar of strawberries. Rory would smile and get lost in his memories, only to have to refocus again. He would make things right and court Dallis starting tomorrow. Sheffield sent word to him that his investment had already doubled, and Rory would have a payout soon. Then his father's debt would shrink and he would be able to spoil his mother and sister more. In a matter of time, he could propose to Dallis. In the meantime, Rory would court her as she deserved, dance with her at balls, and let every gentleman of the ton know she was his. He wouldn't tolerate for any slander against her name. Rory also realized he had one more matter to take care of tomorrow.

After that, no gentleman's name would be attached to Dallis but his own.

Chapter Fourteen

When Rory arrived at Lady Ratcliff's townhome, Shaw delivered him to a private chamber in the back of the house. He stood near the doors leading out into the gardens, waiting for Dallis. Lady Ratcliff entered the room instead. She gave him a stern look, settling into the chair behind her small writing desk. A sense of foreboding filled the air as she regarded him. Dallis's grandmother didn't make him wait long before she spoke.

"I thought over time you would appreciate the special gift of Dallis. She is a treasure to be handled with care. Yet, you break her time and time again. I first thought you were a fortune hunter after her inheritance. Then I met your mother and realized you were too proud to be that kind of man. I began to see how deeply you cared for Dallis. Now I sit here and ponder, perhaps he does not care for her at all? Was he only trying to toy with her emotions, so that she would lower her guard for his pleasure?"

"You are mistaken."

"Am I? I may be old, but I remember what transpires when a gentleman lures you into a darkened corner. But when said gentleman does not call on my granddaughter the next day, I doubt his intentions. Every time you are alone with Dallis, you lead her down a path of indiscretions and then do not call to court her."

The lecture from Dallis's grandmother was worse than any Rory ever received from his own mother. Perhaps because Lady Ratcliff spoke the truth. Any explanation he might have had for yesterday did not excuse his earlier behavior. He'd treated Dallis in a most reprehensible way. How could he convince Lady Ratcliff of his intentions when his actions had spoken otherwise? Rory figured he would need to grovel at Dallis's feet this morning. Instead, he may not be given the opportunity. Still, he needed to try.

"There was a family matter of grave importance which needed my attention yesterday. The day ended before I had a chance to send Dallis an apology. I never meant not to contact her. That is why I am here today. To begin a proper courtship, with your permission."

"No."

"Will you at least give me a chance to defend myself? Ask Dallis if she even wants to see me, then decide."

"My granddaughter came to breakfast with dark circles underneath her eyes. Do you know why?"

"She did not sleep?"

"No, she did not. Dallis cried all night. How is it, that I know this? Because I stood outside her bedroom door and listened to her sorrow. It was then I decided I will not allow you near her again. I will continue to push the courtship with Lord Holdenburg."

"No!" Rory's temper hovered on the edge of exploding.

"You, young man have no opinion in this matter. Now, you need to take your leave. Shaw will escort you to the door. Please do not press this issue. I do not want to involve your mother. I have taken to her friendship and do not wish to offend her. However, I will if you continue to hurt Dallis with your actions."

Rory could do nothing more than honor her request. It didn't mean he would stop his pursuit of Dallis. It only meant he would retreat and use reinforcements. He'd wanted to pursue this relationship on his own, but it would appear he now needed his friends to help him. On his departure from the Ratcliff home he glanced in each room along the hallway for any sign of Dallis. Rory breathed in the fragrance of strawberries floating in the air. Dallis was near. However, his search was useless, for he didn't catch a glimpse of her before Shaw showed him out the door.

~~~~~

"There you are, Nanna. I have searched the house for you. Why are you sitting alone in here?"

"I needed to write some correspondence. Since you were in the garden reading, I thought to write to your mama."

"Please do not tell her, Nanna."

"I won't, my dear. However, I will need to inform her of your progress this season. She will be most impressed to learn that Lord Holdenburg calls on you."

"We are only friends."

"Yes, but your mama has no knowledge of that, only I."

Dallis trusted her grandmother to only tell Mama what she wanted to hear. Nanna was a grand storyteller in her own right. She would regale Mama with stories to make it appear as if Dallis was the belle of the ton. Which was far from true. Before long, Mama would catch wind of her ruination at the hands of Lord Roderick Beckwith. The rumors always reached Inverness. They took a few weeks, but nonetheless they were heard. For now Dallis was safe from her mother's wrath, but soon Mother would order her home and force her to wed a local boy. All because Lord Roderick Beckwith found entertainment in trifling with Dallis's emotions.

Tears came to her eyes as she fought her sadness. Dallis told herself that she would forget Rory and that he no longer held her heart. Try as she might Dallis had found it enormously difficult to erase him from her mind let alone her heart. But as each minute ticked by and he didn't show, it became easier. Before long Lord Rory Beckwith would be but a faint memory. Dallis sniffed and wiped at the tears, trying to avoid Nanna's gaze.

Her eyes landed on a jar of fruit on her grandmother's desk. A peculiar place for it to be. As Dallis drifted closer, she saw a note tied around the top. Before she could reach for the jar, her grandmother grabbed it and hid it behind her back. Nanna's actions triggered her curiosity.

"Nanna, why is there a fruit jar in here?"

"A gift from an acquaintance."

"Which acquaintance?"

"Nobody I have introduced you to. Can you call Shaw? I need help to my room. The pain of one of my headaches is coming on."

Her nanna groaned, closing her eyes in agony. If Dallis didn't know any better, she would think her grandmother faked her illness. But when she noticed the redness of her cheeks, and the pinch around her lips, Dallis felt poorly of her thoughts. She rushed from the room, calling for Shaw.

Soon the servants helped Nanna to bed. When Dallis offered to sit with her, her grandma assured her that she only needed to rest. Feeling a sense of rejection and not knowing what to do with herself, Dallis headed into the kitchen to bake. Perhaps Nanna would enjoy eating some cake when she awakened. When Dallis's moods were troubled, cooking helped to relax her. She could think of no better time to cook than now. The cook helped Dallis to gather the ingredients and utensils. Soon they were baking and the cook shared secrets on how to make the cake moist. Before long Dallis's troubles melted away as she mixed the batter. Each stroke settled her emotions and she focused on enjoying the moment. Forgotten were the tender kisses, the gentle touch, and the passion that simmered beneath the surface when they were together.

It was when Cook and Dallis relaxed, drinking their tea, that Dallis remembered those moments. When reaching for the sugar bowl, Dallis noticed the jar from Nanna's desk. It wasn't just any jar of fruit, but a jar of strawberries. When the cook checked on the cake, Dallis slid the note from the jar and opened the small piece of paper.

Dallis,

I stole these from our garden. I hope they bring you pleasure.

Rory

He came. When? Dallis lifted the jar and turned it over and over in her hand, a smile gracing her lips, realizing the gift was meant for her and held proof of his true intentions. He came with a gift to court her and Nanna sent him away. Dallis couldn't be cross with her grandmother, because she'd only meant to guard Dallis from any more heartache. But Rory *came*. It was enough for Dallis.

She slid the note inside her shoe before the cook returned to the table. Dallis then convinced the cook to make a strawberry glaze for the cake. They prepared a scrumptious cake to share with her grandmother—minus the strawberries for her, because Dallis detested them. She liked the scent for her soap, but the taste was one she could do without. After the cake finished baking and cooled off, Dallis cut a slice and wrapped it in some cloth. When Cook wasn't watching, Dallis directed a footman to deliver the gift to Lord Beckwith. Then she waited for her nanna to awake to serve her the delicious treat.

It was time for everybody to stop interfering. It was her life and who she decided to love was her own choice. Not those of others. And she chose Rory Beckwith.

~~~~~

Dallis waited for Nanna to wake from her nap before she went to her room. She carried in their afternoon tea. The cake with the strawberry glaze rested on the tray, the strawberries sliding off as she walked toward the bed. Still, the effect was all that mattered.

"Does your head still ache?"

Dallis put the tray on the bedside table and poured a cup, adding two spoons of sugar. As she stirred the tea, she watched Nanna eye the cake in suspicion. When her grandmother didn't comment on the strawberries, Dallis realized she would need to say something.

"I made your favorite cake. Cook had those strawberries on the table, so I convinced her to teach me how to make the strawberry glaze you love."

Dallis slid the plate on the bed for her grandmother to enjoy the cake. Nanna watched her, waiting for a reaction, but so did Dallis. When Nanna took a bite of cake, Dallis said her piece.

"You had no right to keep Rory's gift from me. Also, I talked to Shaw. He told me Rory arrived earlier this morning wishing to call on me, but you spoke to him instead. From what I gather, you ran him off. Am I correct in this assumption?"

Lady Ratcliff kept eating her cake, feeling only slightly guilty with the truth. Dallis was correct, but she didn't regret sending the boy away. Since Dallis arrived in town and laid her eyes upon Roderick Beckwith, the girl's moods had been nothing but highs and lows. First she was optimistic that the lord would call on her, and every time he didn't show, she watched Dallis's heart break. Yesterday was the final draw. If Lord Beckwith wouldn't be man enough to court Dallis properly, then he wouldn't step foot in this house again. Lady Ratcliff continued to eat the cake, down to the last bite. The boy *did* deliver worthy strawberries. She would have to hand it to him for that sake alone.

"Well, do you have anything to say for yourself?"

"You are correct, my dear."

"Well?"

"Well what, Dallis? He does not deserve you. Lord Beckwith has had ample enough time to court you, but has yet to make an attempt. Instead he involves your name in multiple scandals. Both of you are very lucky nobody saw your antics at the theater."

"You saw?" Horrified, Dallis sat in the chair near the window.

"No, I saw nothing. But you have confirmed my suspicions with that blush across your cheeks. I will tell you the same as I told your young man—I was young once myself and I know what happens in darkened corners."

"Still Nanna, why did you send him away?"

"Every tear you shed breaks my heart. I convinced your mama to send you here for a season with the intention of finding you a husband worthy of you. Not for a scoundrel to embroil you in a scandal and to send you back home in shame."

"Those are my tears to experience. My heartache to live. I have faith in Rory. He must have his own reasons for his absences."

"Humph."

"I am giving you the courtesy of knowing that I will visit Lady Beckwith this afternoon with the intention of seeing Rory. I will take my maid, Helen, as a chaperone. But you will not come with me. There have been enough distractions between Rory and myself, and no longer will there be."

"Dear, there is much you do not know of your beau. Tread carefully, for you might not like what you discover of him. There are secrets he harbors to protect his mother and sister."

"His secrets will be for him to share with me in his own time. All I know is how he makes me feel and I trust him to do right by me. Your support is all that I seek, not your hindrance."

"I only stopped him out of love for you."

"I understand, Nanna, and I love you for it. However, it is my life to live."

~~~~~~

Rory only visited the Scuffle in the evenings for a good fight. However, after his discussion with Lady Ratcliff, he decided the only way to vent his anger was to beat the living hell out of an opponent. Also, with the dilemma that he was forced to deal with yesterday, he need the extra blunt. Would life ever work to his advantage?

He strolled through the brothel and down the stairs into the fighting area. He walked into the office and sat across from the owner, Madame Bellerose. Most men only knew of the brothel above. But Belle granted other patrons with deeper pockets access to place bets on the outcome of the fights. He first heard of the fighting arena through the Duke of Sheffield one afternoon at Lord Hartridge's. Sheffield knew of the scandal involving his father and his low funds. He'd suggested Belle's out of respect to Rory's opinions on some research projects he funded for Lord Hartridge.

The first time Rory met Belle, she tried to persuade him to visit one of her girls, but he didn't frequent brothels for sport. Rory only carried on relationships with widows, or ladies who had been ruined and preferred to stay unmarried. Belle herself could tempt any man, but she never took part in the profession that made her a profit. Rumor was she carried a torch for a lost love. Whoever the bloke may be, he was a fool for letting her go. She was a beauty with a grace that intensified her attractions. Once again she draped her body in a creation to make men drool. Spilled into a midnight blue gown, her every curve was on display. Belle winked at him while directing Ned to take bets on the next fight.

"You are earlier than usual, Beckwith."

"I need to release some frustration."

"A girl or your father's mess?"

Rory's laugh held a bitter edge. "Both."

"Who is she? Anybody I know?"

"Lady Dallis MacPherson."

"A real beauty, I'm told. Also, there is a rumor about how you have already fought over her name."

"I was defending my sister and Lady Dallis's honor."

"Are the other rumors true?"

Rory slumped further in the chair. "Perhaps."

"When will you men learn? First Wildeburg, then Sheffield, and now you. Who is next?"

"What do we need to learn?"

"How not to ruin perfectly innocent ladies with your prowess. What has frustrated you today that brings you here to fight?"

"Her grandmother Lady Ratcliff warned me away."

"Oh, a dragon she is. I understand. Who do you want, Brutus or Magnus?"

"Magnus."

"Are you sure? The last time he nearly ripped you in two."

"Definitely."

Belle sighed, regarding Lord Roderick Beckwith. The first time they met, her heart gave a flitter-flutter. Her devotion stayed strong to her lost love, but Rory warmed her insides with his sweet smile. He was a cut above the men who frequented her establishment. Most of her customers were jaded rascals who only wanted a good time. However, Rory wanted no part of the underbelly of London's society. He only visited her place to fight. And he only fought because his father left his family broke when he died. Not only broke, but bill collectors beat at his door daily, if the rumors were true. Rory tried his best to shield his mother and sister from their dire circumstances. But when you don't have enough money to pay your servants, women always found out.

Sheffield had vouched for Rory's character and the doll could fight with the best of them. Rory was never one to lose. Sometimes he even took rough beatings, other times he would knock them out with one punch. He was profitable to her business. Belle never turned away money, and she welcomed him whenever he wanted to fight.

She could tell this time Rory wasn't here for the money, but to burn off some steam. And if she wasn't mistaken, perhaps a little sexual frustration. There was much talk about the lovely lady from Scotland. However, before the girl could make a splash amongst the ton, Rory had been attached to her name in the most scandalous of acts. First there was a punch to Lord Phipps for attempting to kiss her. Then there was the drunken kiss on the stoop of her grandparent's townhome. And the last rumor was that while a guest of Lord Holdenburg at the theater, Rory sat with Lady Dallis in a darkened corner. Everybody knew what happens in those darkened seats in a box. Scandalous things to make any woman blush.

Belle nodded. "Good luck. And Rory …"

"Yes?"

"If you need any assistance with Lady Dallis, perhaps I can help."

Rory laughed. "I have had all the help I can get. No, I will win her hand on my own. Plus, I heard of the fiasco with Sheffield and Sophia. While I have ruined Lady Dallis, no offense, I will not sully her name by bringing her to a brothel."

"None taken, dear."

Rory headed toward the boxing ring and watched the fight taking place. The two men were battling over the bed of a courtesan upstairs. Each young pup wanted exclusive rights to her boudoir. He wanted to laugh, for Belle allowed no man those rights. After the fight ended, both men would end up a loser. Belle would collect her winnings from the bout before she disappointed the victor. Rory disrobed to where he only wore his trousers, and sitting on the bench he discarded his boots and socks. He liked to fight in his bare feet. He could grip the floor better this way. Also, it gave him a more primitive feel to the sport.

Ned called his name, then Magnus. The crowd erupted when they found out who fought next. Rory loosened his muscles, stretching and bouncing on his feet as Magnus walked the ring glaring at him. The Scottish brute wanted revenge from their previous fight. Magnus almost beat him, Rory's body left bruised and beaten where he couldn't fight for two weeks. But at the end of the fight Rory elbowed him in the back in the right spot before punching Magnus in the side. It dropped the giant to his knees, which gave Rory the advantage. Then Rory proceeded to pound him in the face over and over until Magnus dropped. Ever since, the man wanted to fight him again, but Belle kept them apart. Today, though, Rory needed to fight Magnus. Rory bristled with an anger he never felt before. Dallis was out of his grasp after this morning. Plus, Rory's mother discovered the true depths of her husband's infidelity and Kathleen was in a mood ever since the theater. His mother knew of his father's demise in the bed of his mistress. But she had been unaware of the countless string of mistresses his father kept throughout their marriage. And to top off his women troubles, Sheffield sent word of a delay in payment. Rory was ready to bash in some heads.

Once he finished with Magnus, perhaps he could convince Belle to let him fight Brutus too.

"Ye dead."

"You can try, you Scottish heathen."

Never call a six-foot-five giant a heathen, especially a Scot. Before Rory was aware what happened he was lying flat on his back. Stars flitted across his eyes and his head pounded. The roar of the crowd cleared his head as they chanted his name. Then he heard the big beast laughing. Rory rose to lean on his elbows, shaking his head to clear the stars away. He watched Magnus strutting around the ring in victory. Lifting his hands above his head in a winning salute. Rory glared at the brute, rising to his feet. The knock onto his ass infuriated him. Not only at his opponent, but with himself. The crowd cheered when they noticed he wasn't down for the count. Magnus turned to see for himself and growled. Rory only smiled at him, holding his hands out and motioning for Magnus to come closer.

Magnus came after him swinging. Rory ducked the punch and landed one in Magnus's side right under the rib cage. Rory knew where to hit an opponent to render them helpless. However, Magnus held more muscle on him than most fighters and would take longer to knock down. Rory took swings at the giant, beating out his frustrations one punch after another. Each time Magnus tried to punch him, Rory would sway and duck out of the way. His energy was intensified by all the injustices handed his way lately. Before long Magnus was weakened by the brute force of Rory's punches. Blood poured from Rory's knuckles mixed with Magnus's blood from the open wounds Rory inflected. Out of nowhere Magnus threw a punch knocking and pinning Rory against the ropes, the beast growling trying to repay him with the same brute force. Rory had enough of being pushed around by everybody in his life and used that as incentive to shove Magnus away. He swung back his arm and leveled a punch to the side of

Magnus's head, dropping him to the floor. Magnus lay still, not moving. Rory leaned on the ropes and gasped for breath with sweat dripping down his face. Still the brute didn't move, the only thing coming from him were deep moans. After a minute, Ned lifted Rory's arm declaring him the winner. There were more groans than cheers—the spectators didn't bet in his favor, wanting him to lose. Which was fine with Rory, earning more of a cut from Belle's profit. Ned dragged Magnus from the ring with help from Belle's guards.

As Rory laced his boots, Belle offered him a towel.

"Do you feel any better, Rory?"

"No."

"Do you want another fight?"

"No, they will not solve my problems."

"Then what?"

"I try again tomorrow, then the next, until I can see her."

"And your other problems?"

"One day at a time, Belle."

He finished getting dressed, then collected his winnings and left the seedier side of London to the vultures who thrived in it. A life that had ruined his family and one he never wanted a part of, but he would endure for the time being to help them survive.

And so that his sister never had to know about their father's disgrace.

Chapter Fifteen

Dallis enjoyed tea with Lady Beckwith and Rory's sister. They enlightened her on stories from his childhood. It was during one tale, when she was laughing so hard with tears in her eyes, that she heard his voice. She wiped her eyes, waiting impatiently for Rory to join them. However, after a half an hour, he still didn't come into the parlor. She tried to be polite and talk, but kept getting distracted at every noise. When another half hour passed with no sign of Rory, Dallis decided she needed to leave. She had overstayed her welcome. Also, the looks of pity she received from his mother and sister almost had Dallis in tears of a different sort. She thought to confide in Lady Beckwith about her feelings for her son, but couldn't bring herself to speak. Dallis feared that Lady Beckwith would inform her that Rory didn't share those same feelings toward her. She had reached her limit on rejection today. Dallis made the decision to take her leave and try another tactic tomorrow. She would see if Sidney or Sophia had any valuable advice.

After Dallis left the Beckwith home, Kathleen shared her thoughts with her mother concerning Lady Dallis.

"Mama, she came for Rory. Why did he not join us?"

"I know, dear, my heart breaks for her. It is time I have a word with my son regarding Lady Dallis. I do not understand why Rory has stayed away."

"Let me, Mama. I can inquire as a friend of Lady Dallis, not as a mother harassing him to marry."

"You are probably correct, my dear. Do make a point with him that if he does not have an interest in Dallis, then Lord Holdenburg would be more than pleased to make her his bride."

Kathleen felt a sense of loss at her mother's threat for her brother. While she wanted Rory to marry Dallis, she also wanted happiness for her new friend—and at this moment she wasn't happy. If would serve Rory right, if Lady Dallis became engaged to Lord Holdenburg, since he had been dragging his feet. Perhaps then Rory would see what he was on the verge of losing and chase Lady Dallis. But Kathleen's own sadness was more than that. Something else wiggled in her heart at the thought of Lord Holdenburg getting married.

It must be because she detested the man and didn't want to see him happy with anybody, especially Dallis.

~~~~~

Rory sunk into the bath, sighing as the hot water comforted his pains. His body ached from where Magnus threw him on the floor. He lowered his fists into the water and winced when the sting burned across his knuckles. He was in a sorry shape and grateful that he didn't need to escort his mother or Kathleen to any ball this evening. Rory heard them entertaining in the parlor, but he was in no mood to be civil to anybody. Rory needed to recuperate before he presented himself in front of his mother. If he would have joined them, she would have known instantly of his pain. No, it was for the best to appear rude and pretend ignorance of any visitors.

As he rose from the tub, he dripped water on the floor. Walking to the bed with the towel wrapped around his waist he saw that Agnes had whipped him up a batch of the soothing medication for his hands. While it smelled atrocious, it did the trick. The few servants under his employ knew of his fighting to hold the household together, and kept the truth from his mother. He rubbed the ointment on his knuckles and sighed with relief as the sting disappeared from the comforting gel. Once he felt relief, he dressed and sat in the chair near the fireplace. It was an old chair which looked worse for wear, but it was his favorite. Sometimes when he sat in it, he could focus on his dilemmas and come to a conclusion on how to solve them.

Only this time there were no solutions. Rory's life was spinning out of control and he had no handle on how to stop it. Before now, he was a sensible fellow who approached life with clear thoughts and lived on the straight and narrow. Granted, when he was younger, he had his fair scrapes of trouble. But ever since Lord Hartridge took him under his wing, Rory became determined to make something of his life. To provide for his family in a way his father never did. To do that, he became respectable, knowledgeable, courteous, and everything a lady would admire. But once Dallis entered his life, one look at her and all rational thoughts flew out the door. Rory fell off the path and headed down dead ends which never led them to her. Always further away. He leaned his head back and closed his eyes, trying to figure a way to see Dallis without her grandmother knowing.

When Rory opened his eyes, it was to discover his sister had snuck into his room and sat cross-legged on his bed. Another lady he seemed to fail. He slid his hands to his sides, hiding the bruising. Kathleen eyed him with a quizzical look.

"It was very rude of you not to join us for tea. Mama is most disappointed with you."

"Not tonight, sister."

"It is either me, or Mama herself wants to talk to you."

Rory released a breath. "Spill it, squirt. I have business I need to attend to."

"You missed Dallis."

Rory sat forward. "When?"

"She came to visit during afternoon tea. I think she hoped to see you. Anyway she left—and looked to be near tears too."

Rory stood, running his hands through his hair, pacing back and forth across his bedroom. She came here for him. Damn. If only he had walked into the parlor and he would have seen her for himself. He *had* to find a way past her protective grandmother. Perhaps he should take a page out of Wildeburg's book? If he snuck into her room tonight, he could explain his absence. Then maybe steal a kiss or two. First, he had to get rid of Kathleen.

"Mama also wanted me tell you that if you do not make a stand for Dallis, she will persuade Lord Holdenburg to ask for Dallis's hand in marriage. She thinks they make a sweet couple. If you want my opinion ..."

"I do not."

"Well ..."

"Good night, Kathleen."

Rory managed to extract his sister off his bed and guide her toward the door. Kathleen kept rattling on about Lord Holdenburg and Dallis, not making much sense to him. His thoughts were focused on his plans to see Dallis. Would she have on the same white nightgown that displayed her curves? Would her hair lay unbound, flowing around her shoulders? Could he tempt her into a few kisses? Rory hoped that all the answers to his questions would be yes.

"Rory!"

"What?"

Kathleen stopped in her tracks, making him stop too. If he continued, he would only be dragging her to the door. Rory didn't want to hurt her, he only wanted her gone. Kathleen's fingers tried to peel his hand away from her arm. He grimaced in pain when her nails scraped against an open sore.

"Who did you fight? And why?"

"It is none of your business."

"It is, if this is the result."

"Kathleen ..."

"Tell me or I will tell Mama."

"I needed to let off a bit of steam."

"Did you win?"

Rory laughed, "Yes."

"How much did you win?"

"It was only for sport."

"Rory, I am well aware of how you earn money to support our family. I have for quite some time. Papa left us broke, didn't he?"

"Kathleen, this is my burden to carry."

"When will you realize it is also mine?"

"Never. It is my duty to protect and provide for you. You are meant to enjoy the life you were born into. I only wish I could provide better for you."

In that moment Kathleen finally understood the sacrifices Rory suffered for her. And the only way to repay his generosity would be to find a way to bring coin into their home. Kathleen either would need to wed, or do what her father did best. And that was cards. Her father taught her how to play with the best of them. Kathleen knew every trick in the book and then a few that she learned herself. If Rory could fight to bring in extra money, then she must find some card games to play. Kathleen heard of a place near Vauxhall Gardens where the ladies wore masks to hide their identities. It was an exclusive club only for the well-privileged with deep pockets. She only needed to secure an invitation. After that, she would win the huge pots at the tables.

She stood on her tiptoes and brushed a kiss across his cheek. "You are the best brother any girl could ever hope for. Now, for me to be the best sister, I will take my leave so that you can go to Dallis. Do not keep her waiting any longer."

Once Kathleen left, he ran to his study. Rory needed to send a payment to the grocer before his mother found out about their past due bill. He wrote a note and stuck some cash into an envelope to leave with Agnes. On his way out of the room he spotted a wrapped linen parcel on the edge of his desk. A strong scent of strawberries wafted in the air as he pulled the cloth apart. There resting inside was a piece of cake with strawberry glaze. A smile spread across his face, realizing the gift was from Dallis. She knew about his visit. She must have come today in hopes to repair her grandmother's tongue. He took a bite out of the cake and moaned in pleasure. The strawberries tasted divine. Just like her. Rory continued to eat the cake as he left. He was on his way to her, now that he knew it wasn't too late.

He should wait until tomorrow to see Dallis, and do it properly. However, not one minute of their relationship was proper thus far, so why start now?

Chapter Sixteen

Dallis rested on the window seat with the pane cracked open. A cool breeze wafted in turning the room chilly. The cold went unnoticed as she stared into the dark night. Stars lit the sky, reminding Dallis of childhood stories of how the stars guided the warrior's home after their long battles. Dallis made a wish on the first star she saw. The act was foolish, but all the same she tried. Somewhere in the universe something hopefully would make her dreams come true. She traced a pattern on the window, picturing her wish. She imagined Rory's passion-filled eyes as he enticed her into his arms. Lost in her fantasy, Dallis wasn't aware the window had opened wider and he hung onto her windowsill.

Dallis gasped, "Rory?" She wondered if she only imagined him.

"Dallis."

"Are you real?"

"As real as you wish me to be."

Dallis reached out to touch him. Her palm curved around his cheek feeling his warmth. He was real—and he hung from her window. How? She reached to pull him in and he lost his grasp, hanging on with one hand. The muscles in his arm bulged through his shirt as he gripped the sill. She cried his name in fear.

"Shh, love. Before you awaken your grandmother. I want to live."

"But you are about to fall."

"Stand back, honey," he ordered, swinging his body. He pushed the window open further and tumbled inside. He made enough of a racket to wake the dead. Lucky for him, her grandmother was a sound sleeper. Dallis prayed that none of the servants saw Rory either. Or else her reputation *would* definitely be ruined and she would be sent home to wed a groom hand-picked by her father.

"You know, love, you are a sight for sore eyes. You are wearing exactly what I hoped you would be."

"Do not call me your love, Rory Beckwith."

"Ahh, but you are."

"Are you drunk again?"

"Come here." He laid on his back, smiling at her, and crooked his finger.

She shook her head and backed away.

"You need to leave right this instant."

"After I get a kiss."

"No! Now."

Rory hooked his finger on the hem of her nightgown and tugged. Dallis lost her balance and fell right where he wanted her to—in his arms.

"Mmm, now this is better."

"You, Rory Beckwith, are a scoundrel of the highest order."

"I only want one kiss, Dallis."

"Then after you get your kiss, you will want more. All the while, my reputation will be torn to tatters and where will you be? But absent as always."

The tone of Dallis's voice saddened as she reprimanded him. He hurt her deeply by staying away. Rory never meant her any harm. At first he thought she deserved better than him, after that it was one crisis after another which prevented him from courting her. Rory came tonight to declare his intentions and perhaps steal only a kiss or two. Maybe three, because she felt so delightful in his arms. All right, four, then he would leave.

However, after the fourth kiss, he didn't stop. He lost count how many times he sampled her delicious lips. The kisses turned to soft caresses as he slid her nightgown up. Her body was softer than any silk. The aroma of strawberries inflamed his senses. He wanted more from Dallis. Rory wanted to strip her bare and lay with her as he kissed her everywhere. Long slow kisses that lasted a lifetime.

Dallis swore she wouldn't let him anywhere near her again. But when she fell into his arms, it was as if she fell into home. His embrace gave her a sense of security. His kisses made her crave him. They set her on fire with a need for Rory to show her what happens when passion ignites. The cool breeze caressed her legs as he tugged the nightgown around her hips. Rory's fingers stroked across her buttocks, pulling Dallis into his hardness, and she released a moan.

He pulled her core into him and rotated his hips. His cock was hard and aching to be inside her. Rory wanted to slide into her warmth and lose himself forever. When she moved her hips along with his, he almost spent himself. His Dallis was a fast learner. He couldn't wait to teach her how wonderful they could be together. He rolled her over so that Dallis lay underneath him. Rory saw the desire shining from her eyes and knew Dallis wanted him too. When he slid his hand between her thighs she opened for him. Rory's hand moved higher and his fingers sunk into her wetness, and her eyes darkened into a deep forest of green. As he slid inside her core, she closed her eyes and moaned with pleasure. This time he'd promised only one kiss, but his need to savor Dallis replaced all common sense.

Rory kissed a trail along her legs until he reached her wetness. He spread her thighs apart, dipping his head in for a nibble. Ahh, the temptation of strawberries whetted his appetite, his tongue sliding slowly across her wetness. Dallis moaned his name as he went in for another taste. Rory could no more stop at one kiss than he could stop breathing. His tongue stroked in and out of her wetness as his thumb flicked across her clit. He wanted Dallis to come undone under his mouth. He slid his tongue out and flicked it back and forth across her hard clit, coaxing her to lose control. Dallis's body tensed underneath him.

Rory's mouth did the most delicious acts. She never wanted him to stop and held back her screams as he pleasured her with his mouth. Her hips pressed against his mouth as he continued to drive her over the edge. Dallis held on, wanting Rory to ease her ache. And when he started to use his mouth and fingers on her wetness, she lost control. Dallis's body flew over the edge, his kisses dominating her senses.

Rory caught Dallis as he brought her to her fullest pleasure. Dallis's body went soft in his arms. Her hair tumbled around them, the red strands dark alongside the white of his shirt. When she lifted her eyes to him, her real beauty blew him away.

"You are so beautiful, Dallis."

She blushed, shaking her head in denial. Dallis knew she held no true beauty, not the kind that made men fall at her feet. But she felt special from Rory's attentions—from his looks, to this touch, to the kisses he bestowed upon her body. How could she not feel beautiful when he worshipped her? She only hoped this latest episode wouldn't result like the other ones. Dallis couldn't take any more heartache.

"Do not hurt me anymore, Roderick Beckwith. I could not stand it, if you do."

"Ah, love. Please allow me to explain."

"No, I will not listen to your excuses. I only want you present. If you cannot be, then I will return to Scotland."

"No!" His voice rose as he rolled her over again. "You are not leaving me."

"Then give me a reason to stay."

"Don't cry, Dallis. I am a fool."

Tears streamed down Dallis's cheeks as he wiped his fingers across them. He leaned over and gently pressed a kiss on her lips.

"I love you, Dallis MacPherson."

"How? You do not even know my character."

"I know all that I need to, and I will learn the rest after we wed."

"Wed? You cannot even court me properly," Dallis scoffed.

"You want to be courted? I will show you courting, my lady." He pulled Dallis up, sliding her nightgown back into place.

Rory stepped away from Dallis, causing a void. The loss would only be for a short time. He would give her a courtship to make her swoon.

"Well, consider this to be the first round of courting, my dear."

"This is not appropriate courting, Lord Beckwith. This is your final chance to ruin me."

"Ahh, Dallis that is not fair."

"Humph. Good night, Lord Beckwith. I do not want to set eyes upon you unless it is proper."

"How am I supposed to court you, when your grandmother has forbidden me to cross her doorstep?"

"You appear to be a clever fellow. I am sure you will think of something. Now leave." Dallis pointed to the window.

"Ah, lass, you drive a hard bargain, but one I am game for." He gave her a quick peck before he escaped out the window.

Dallis smiled, watching him disappear into the darkness. She'd only pretended to be disappointed with him, because she enjoyed it when he teased her. Her excitement grew, anticipating what he had planned for tomorrow. How would Rory convince Nanna to let him court her? Rory didn't know that Dallis had warned Nanna off interfering.

Perhaps, Dallis should have Nanna make Rory fight to enter.

Chapter Seventeen

Dallis waited in the parlor as Shaw escorted some of their last guests to the door. Teatime was over and as usual Rory didn't show. She rested in her chair, attempting to keep a serene smile in place as Nanna's oldest friend, Lady Farnsworth, still remained. Dallis's temper brimmed near the surface. The next time she came upon Lord Roderick Beckwith he would realize the full extent how finished she was with him. She'd decided this morning not to involve Nanna in her playful ploy. For which she was glad. If Nanna thought Rory would arrive, and he didn't, she would either confront Lady Beckwith on the scandalous behavior of her son or force Dallis's return to Scotland. When Dallis threatened Nanna the day before, she'd walked a thin line. If Nanna proved herself correct, there would be no recourse for Dallis.

She heard Shaw returning, and he was not alone. Dallis heard multiple footsteps nearing the parlor. She turned her head to the door and the new guests arriving surprised her. Not only did Rory come, but he brought his mother and sister with him. When their eyes met, he leaned against the doorjamb and raised his eyebrows in confidence. He'd outwitted her grandmother, it seemed, using his family as a decoy. Rory was a devious one, and she would need to keep on her toes. Dallis sent him a nod for a job well done. However, Rory wasn't finished with his point, strolling to her grandmother's side and presenting her with a jar of strawberries to prove it. Her nanna shot him a shrewd look, and then one over to Dallis. Dallis shrugged her innocence.

Kathleen sat near Dallis and his mother joined Lady Ratcliff and Lady Farnsworth on the sofa. Rory had seen the astonishment on Dallis's face when they entered. His girl held no faith in his making an appearance. He'd deliberately waited until near the end of afternoon tea before making their arrival. Rory didn't want to share Dallis with any other suitors or busy-bodies of the ton. He'd made a grand gesture when he handed her grandmother the strawberries. It was also a warning to her nanna that he meant to court Dallis and wouldn't let anybody stand in his way. Her grandmother looked him over and, for only him to see, gave a nod of approval.

Rory then stood by the fireplace and watched Dallis and Kathleen chat animatedly. Soon they were in a fit of giggles, his sister explaining about an incident at a musical she'd attended this week. Then his mother called Kathleen over to the sofa to show off her new dress. He regretted his tone with her the previous evening and took Kathleen shopping this morning. Rory had a few extra coins left over from the fight and wanted to buy Kathleen a new dress rather than having her wear last year's rags.

Which left him alone with Dallis for a moment.

He slid into the chair Kathleen had occupied. Crossing one leg over the other, with a lazy expression he regarded Dallis. Rory watched the blush grace her cheeks with his intense regard. Pure loveliness. He could gaze upon her all day long. Soon he would be able to. The profits from Sheffield's investment should flow through any day now.

"You look lovely today, Lady Dallis."

"Thank you, Lord Beckwith."

"Would you like to take a walk around your grandmother's garden?"

"No, sir, I think it would be best if we stay chaperoned."

"Ah, dear, you are no fun. I hope you loosen up before we wed."

"We will not wed until you properly court me, my lord."

"Is that not what I am doing today, my lady?"

"Do you usually court young ladies with your mother and sister?"

"Only if I need ammunition to cross the threshold."

Dallis laughed at his description of strategy. She had to give him credit for his sly thinking. The ladies turned at her laughter, which only made her blush even more. Then her grandmother urged Lady Farnsworth to leave, reminding her of a previous engagement. When Nanna's friend left, she ordered Shaw to close the door on his way out.

"I am glad you have accompanied your son today, Lady Beckwith. You have saved me the trouble of calling on your kindness. It would appear your son has pressed his suit with my granddaughter in an unsavory manner. While Dallis has been more than a willing participant, it can no longer continue."

"Rory? Is this true?" His mother turned toward him.

Rory nodded. So the grandmother decided to push the issue. Damn her. He wouldn't be able to give Dallis the courtship he wanted to. Lady Ratcliff would force his hand now.

"I am sorry, dear," Rory whispered to Dallis, hoping that she would forgive him.

"Nanna, stop." Dallis understood his gaze and felt the same sorrow. He was attempting to correct his past mistakes by calling on her today. Rory meant to make their courtship fun, but her nanna set to ruin it.

"No, Dallis. Not after what I witnessed last night. Lady Beckwith, your son visited my granddaughter in the dead of night. Sneaking into her bedroom through her window and staying for far longer than necessary. Then I watched him sneak out her window again and escape into the night through my gardens. I kept quiet, because I did not want to wake the servants and cause an alarm and the ruination of Dallis. I am hoping to keep this a quiet, family manner."

Lady Beckwith sat in shock at the allegations. Rory was never one to ruin a young lady. Why would he act this way toward Lady Dallis? Rory was the child that she always depended on, and now it seemed he'd created a mess to clean up. Not that Lady Dallis was a mess, far from it. She was a charming lady who would make a lovely daughter-in-law. However, this wasn't how she planned for her son to wed. Granted, she schemed with Lady Ratcliff earlier in the season to set Rory and Dallis together. Now what they'd planned came to fruition, instead of satisfaction, she sat in embarrassment on how it came to be.

"Rory, do you have anything to say for yourself?" Lady Beckwith questioned him.

"Nothing, it would seem. Lady Ratcliff has proven that I am nothing but a scoundrel chasing under Lady Dallis's skirt."

"Roderick Allan Beckwith, you will apologize now."

"Sorry, Mama. I am frustrated at this situation. May I please have a few private words with Dallis?" he asked Lady Ratcliff.

"I do not think that would be appropriate."

"Well, either you let me talk to her alone, or else what you are hoping to achieve will not come to pass."

"Humph. Lady Beckwith, will you and your daughter like to join me in the garden? There are some roses I would like to show you."

The three ladies left the room, each one of them wearing looks of indecision as they headed toward the garden. Once they were alone, Rory made sure the door was locked. What he wanted to profess to Dallis, he didn't want any disturbance.

Rory knelt at Dallis's feet, gathering her hands in his. He brought them to his mouth and placed a kiss across her knuckles.

"Dallis, my love. I have not courted you properly throughout your season in London. In fact, I have not paid court to you at all. My behavior has been scandalous at best, and I have pretty much ruined your beautiful name, causing doubt on your virtue. All I can promise is that I will spend the rest of my life courting you every day as my wife. Will you do me the honor of becoming my bride?"

Tears flowed from Dallis's eyes. This was not how she'd imagined the season would go. When she arrived in London with the intention of securing a groom, she never thought in her wildest dreams to fall in love with her soul mate. It no longer mattered how their courtship began, as long as she could be with Rory. If this was how they were to marry, at least she could carry in her heart that he wanted her. Perhaps, one day, he would love her truly. Oh, she knew Rory spouted his love for her and kept calling her his "love", but Dallis didn't feel as if he meant the words. Sure, he lusted after her, that was more than obvious, but love? No, she didn't think he understood the word. And even though Dallis loved Rory for the emotions he drew from her, she was not *in love* with him. They hardly knew the truth of each other's characters.

"Dallis?" he asked.

"Yes, Rory, I would be honored to be your bride. And as your wife I will make it your duty to court me every day. There shall be no other approach for you."

Rory laughed, drawing her into his arms, and kissing her gently on the lips. "You have made me the happiest man on earth."

Dallis laughed. "Sorry about Nanna's strong arm."

"I am grateful for your nanna's interference. Now I no longer have to wait to have you in my bed. How long *will* we have to wait?"

Her grandmother's voice startled them. "I expect you to get a special license and wed her within a week. There is talk floating around the ton about your hi-jinks regarding Dallis and I will not have her name slandered any longer. Do I make myself clear, boy?"

Somehow the wily woman unlocked the door and overheard his proposal. Rory would have to always keep one eye on that lady. His mother and Kathleen waited behind Lady Ratcliff in excitement.

"Does two weeks from today meet with your approval, Lady Ratcliff?"

"Yes, it does."

His mother and Kathleen rushed to their side exclaiming how delighted they were to have Dallis join their family. He even received a hug from Lady Ratcliff with a further warning to make Dallis happy or else. The ladies pushed Rory away with their sudden discussions of wedding plans which covered dresses, food, guests, and the venue. Lady Ratcliff offered her home for the ceremony and reception. Everybody understood the reason why even though no words were spoken. A deep shame over his finances took away his thrill on becoming engaged to Dallis.

Rory couldn't even provide for a bride. Let alone a lavish wedding.

His coffers were empty. Dallis would enter into a broke household after she spoke her vows. Rory knew that she was an heiress in her own right, but he wouldn't take a coin from her. She could put her money in a trust for their children and only for them. No, he didn't want this for her, nonetheless it was how things must be. Rory would break the news of his financial situation to Dallis after they wed and then hopefully in time with the investments with Sheffield, he could comfort her in the finest things.

Dallis wanted to stand next to Rory to be near him, but the ladies required her opinion on the wedding arrangements. She didn't care for any of this talk. She only wanted the act over with so they could start their life together. Dallis looked over Kathleen's shoulder at Rory who rested against the wall. She noticed the wistfulness on his face and wondered why. Did he feel forced to wed her? Was she mistaken in his intentions? Did he only wish to fool around with her, not to marry her? When Rory noticed her watching him, he attempted a poor excuse of a smile. It fell flat. Before long he urged his mother and Kathleen to leave. With a kiss to her cheek they left.

"Why, Nanna?"

"It was for the best, my dear. I needed to bring the boy up to scratch. Before long he would have you so ruined, nobody will even call on you. You are lucky Lord Holdenburg still calls. His reputation has kept all the other suitors still seeking your attention."

"I will need to inform Lord Holdenburg of my impending nuptials."

"Better yet, we shall invite him to the ceremony."

"That would not be very gracious."

"Posh, he is an old friend to the Beckwith family. He would expect nothing less."

Dallis listened to her nanna rattle on about who else to invite and what they needed to accomplish over the next couple of weeks. She only replied with half a heart as she kept wondering why Rory appeared so dejected earlier. Dallis knew her parents wouldn't be able to make the trip in time, and it didn't matter to her. They never made time for her in the past, and would only consider this a nuisance. Perhaps she could convince Sheffield to walk her down the aisle? Sheffield had become a good friend when he paid court to her before he wed Sophia. Dallis would pay them a visit tomorrow and ask for his help. Part of her was thrilled to become Rory's bride, but another part of her was left unsatisfied.

She couldn't quite understand why, but hoped to before she walked down the aisle and shared her vows with him.

Chapter Eighteen

Rory spent the entire evening scouring the ledgers for any possible solutions. How could he bring a wife, who had the finest of things, into a household one step away from poverty? It wouldn't take Dallis long to notice how tight their household strings pulled. While it was an unspoken subject with Dallis now, she would inquire when they were married. Still, there was no extra blunt to be found. He needed to pay a visit to Sheffield. Rory was aware of the early morning hour, but he could no longer wait. If he was to bring a bride into his home, then at least he would make it *appear* as if they had the finer things. It was what Dallis deserved.

Sheffield's butler showed him into the study where the duke worked behind his desk. The room was luxurious, which one would expect of a gentleman of Sheffield's station. Rory settled into a large leather chair. Sheffield offered him a cigar, and he declined. Sheffield motioned for his footman to leave and he reclined back, waiting for Rory to speak. With reluctance, Rory explained his situation and humbled himself to ask for Sheffield's help.

"Congratulations. I never thought you would offer."

"Well, it was more of an ultimatum by her grandmother."

"Nonetheless, I wish you many years of happiness. Lady Dallis is a special woman who deserves the very best."

"Which brings me to the point of my visit. Has there been word on our investment?"

"Sorry to say, no. The ship has gotten lost at sea from the strong storms a week ago. The vessel should arrive in port in a few weeks. I can front you a loan until then."

"No, I am already indebted to you enough. I will visit Belle and schedule a few fights during the next week. That should earn me enough to give Dallis a honeymoon. Maybe by the time we return, the ship will arrive."

"Here, let me be of some assistance. As a wedding present, you can have use of our home in Camberley. Whisk Dallis away for a couple of worry-free weeks. Wilde and I will look after your mother and sister."

"Why?"

"Why what?"

"Explain, why are you being so generous after all the trouble I have caused? I beat you to a pulp a few months ago."

"Yes, but you were defending my wife's honor. So, I forgave you on the merit of your upstanding friendship with Sophia. Most men would have turned the other cheek, but not you. And for that I will always owe you a debt of gratitude."

Sheffield's words silenced Rory. Sheffield was a bigger man than he could ever be.

"The gift is more for Dallis. She was a friend who encouraged me to explore my true feelings for Sophia. And for that I am indebted to her too. You realize, once Sophia hears your good news, she will insist on hosting a dinner in your honor?"

"What good news do I need to hear?" Sophia wandered into the study and went to Sheffield's side.

She leaned over to give her husband a passionate kiss. When Rory groaned at their display of affection, she broke away laughing. Sophia rested on the edge of Sheffield's chair, his arm wrapped tight around her waist. Their intimate regard used to embarrass Rory, but now he was immune to them. If it wasn't Sheffield and Sophia in a passionate exchange, it was Wildeburg and Sidney. Both couples were insatiable.

"Rory has proposed to the lovely Lady Dallis, and she has accepted. They will exchange their vows in two weeks."

"Two weeks? Are you mad, Rory Beckwith? How can she plan a wedding in that short amount of time?"

"Her grandmother did not give me an option."

"Oh ..." Sophia replied finally understanding the need to rush. "Why, Rory Beckwith, I did not know you had a naughty streak in you."

"Well, Sophia, I would never have thought the same about you. What one will do for somebody they love."

Sheffield said, "I have offered them the house in Camberley for the use of a honeymoon retreat."

"Oh, that is splendid. You are such the romantic, dear." Sophia placed a kiss on Sheffield's cheek gazing into his eyes. Sheffield's expression turned intimate in nature. It was time for Rory to leave before the room grew any more uncomfortable. He'd solved part of his problem with some help from his friends.

"Thank you both for your generous offer. I will accept, and an invitation should arrive soon. I hope you will join us as our guests for the wedding."

"We would not miss it for the world. Be patient on the other matter. By the time you return from your honeymoon, all will be well," Sheffield assured him.

Rory nodded and left before he had to witness anymore of their affections. While he understood their feelings—for that was how he felt about Dallis—he didn't want to watch. He would stop by Belle's and line up some fights over the next couple of days. He wanted to buy Dallis a ring worthy of her beauty. To achieve that, he need some blunt. After a few fights he would find her something simple but elegant. Later, after he settled his family's legacy into the fortunes they were meant to have, he would purchase a grander ring to display her status to the ton.

~~~~~~~

Dallis waited in the parlor for Sheffield. The butler explained the duke would be with her shortly. She sipped on her tea, taking notice of the grand room. It held a charming elegance that could only come from Sophia. Dallis wanted to be closer friends with the duchess and her friend Sidney, but her grandmother still discouraged the friendship due to the scandalous courtships that led to their marriages. Now that her own marriage to Rory was knee-deep in scandal and they were Rory's close friends, she should get the chance to socialize with them. Dallis had already seen how kind and encouraging they were. Perhaps they held insight to Rory's behavior and could offer an explanation for his standoffishness.

Sophia came into the room followed by Sheffield. A blush spread across the duchess's cheeks, and Sheffield held a secretive smile he kept directing toward his wife. Dallis sensed what those looks meant, for that is how she always appeared after spending time alone with Rory. With Sophia's hair mussed and her dress full of wrinkles so early in the day, it could only be one thing. Their happiness brought joy to Dallis. Sheffield opened his heart in forgiveness to love Sophia, despite the secrets that could have kept them apart.

"I hear congratulations are in order, my dear," said Sheffield.

"My, I did not expect word to travel so fast. I guess it is true what they say of the rumor mills in London."

Sophia laughed. "While that is true, that is not the case with your engagement. Rory left here a short time ago and shared the good news. We are thrilled for you."

"Thank you. May I ask you a favor, Your Grace?"

"Alex. We are friends, Dallis."

"Alex, will you walk me down the aisle? My parents cannot attend the wedding and my grandfather is at his estate."

"It would be my pleasure, my dear."

Sophia said, "Also, Alex has already offered our home in Camberley for your honeymoon. Can you stay for tea, Dallis? I have sent word for Sidney to join us."

"Yes, I hoped to have a word with you regarding Rory."

Sheffield said, "That is my cue to leave. I shall see you soon, Dallis."

"Thank you, Alex, for everything."

Sheffield left after sending his wife another sizzling look. He loved to make Sophia blush. Interruptions from Rory and now Dallis had kept them from spending time alone this morning. Both of them still confused by the other.

In Sheffield's opinion, Rory needed to be honest with Dallis, and until he did Rory would remain a mystery to Dallis. Perhaps, after Rory's finances became more stable, he would stop living his double life.

Otherwise, before long, his secrets would catch up with him and when they did, it wouldn't end well.

Sophia discussed the wedding arrangements with Dallis, inquiring about her dress and the plans that had been made. Soon, Sidney joined them and when told the news she cried out her delight. Rory and Sidney had been close friends for many years and she regarded him as a brother. Sidney exclaimed how she'd known Dallis would be perfect for him and how she'd urged Rory to court her. As they talked Dallis relaxed more in their company and before long she spilled the entire truth of their unconventional courtship. To have friends to confide in lifted a burden of shame off her shoulders. The two ladies laughed and explained about their own courtships. Dallis knew part of the scandal of Sheffield and Sophia, but held no clue to Wildeburg and Sidney's relationship. Dallis laughed along with them, feeling better already. After they drank two pots of tea and ate a plate of biscuits, Dallis had formed a new friendship that she believed would last for years to come. With that feeling, she asked them for advice regarding Rory.

"Rory never would explain, but I hoped one of you might help me understand his hesitation to court me."

Sophia and Sidney exchanged glances. They knew Rory should be the one to explain to Dallis why he didn't court her, but they also knew how proud he was and it would be up to them to explain why. It was the least they could do—to help him enter a marriage without secrets.

"Rory is broke. Pride has been his downfall the entire time," Sidney explained.

"I do not understand. Why should any of that matter?"

"He wanted to come to you as a wealthy man. Not as a man who would be perceived as a fortune hunter," Sophia continued.

Sidney explained more of the details concerning the late Lord Beckwith and how he left his family in debt. That over the last few years Rory struggled to keep his family from debtor's prison. She didn't explain how he earned his money, and admitted she had spoken too much as it was. But Sidney wanted Dallis to understand the burdens he lived with. Sidney hoped that after the wedding Rory wouldn't let his pride still be his downfall. She urged Dallis to break through his defenses after they wed.

Dallis finally put the pieces together. She saw how Rory's pride kept him from courting her. Rory had mentioned that she deserved better, and now she understood. Dallis *had* noticed the threadbare furniture at their home, and Kathleen's dresses came from past fashion plates. Dallis even saw the small staff of servants. But none of that concerned her. She didn't love him for what he had, but for who he was. It was a trait she'd learned from her grandmother. Her nanna gifted her with that feeling and that is how she judged others. Her nanna always loved her for who she was, not who she wanted her to be unlike her own parents. And that was how she loved Rory. For who he was, not for how he provided for her. As long as Dallis had his love, that would be the only thing that mattered. Money comes and money goes, but as long as they had each other, then they would conquer all. She had enough money for them. Dallis understood that he would reject that idea, but hopefully in time she could convince Rory to let her help his family.

"Thank you for explaining Rory's behavior. It has helped me to understand him better. I feared that he regretted being forced to ask for my hand in marriage."

"Dallis, Rory loves you," Sidney said firmly.

"So he professes. But until he can trust me with his secrets, then the scope of his love are only words."

Chapter Nineteen

They spent the days leading to their wedding with not a moment alone. Dallis's fears only strengthened with Rory's dark brooding looks. While his mother, Kathleen and friends' excitement at the impending nuptials should have soothed Dallis, it only fueled her thoughts that Rory regretted his proposal. He was always polite and agreed to every decision made, but Dallis sensed that he wasn't on board with her grandmother's forceful hand. He never tried to steal a kiss or sneak into her room now. Though their courtship was unorthodox, Dallis craved for attention from the Rory who had ruined her.

Rory stood across the room near the window. He stared out at the pounding rain, the weather reflecting his foul mood. He listened to the ladies discussing his upcoming marriage. Dallis's quiet voice agreed to every detail being made. She never put forth her own requests but approved whatever his mother and her grandmother suggested. The tone of her voice drew his attention away from the storm. When he turned, he saw how withdrawn his bride had become. No smile lit her face, and her eyes held a sadness that Rory felt like a punch to his gut. Did she no longer wish to marry him? He'd tried to keep his distance this week and act the proper gentleman he should have the entire time he'd known her. Rory ached to hold Dallis in his arms and kiss her sweet lips. But he had already ruined her name and brought shame onto his family.

When he saw the doubt in Dallis's eyes, Rory knew what he had to do. To hell with propriety. He only needed to make Dallis happy. Everybody and everything else could hang.

"If you ladies would excuse me, I have some business to conclude before we leave on our honeymoon. I will have the carriage return to take you home, Mama."

The ladies assured him they had everything under control and said their goodbyes—except for Dallis. Her lips only pinched more, watching him walking out. He sensed her stare and stopped at the door. Before he left, he winked at her, then continued on to the foyer before she could respond. Rory chuckled, imagining her reaction. Life with her would never be dull.

Along his way to the foyer he took a detour up the stairs to Dallis's room. When he encountered her maid, Helen, in the hallway Rory requested a favor and explained his reasoning. Soon, he had the maid sighing and offering assistance to help sneak Dallis away.

While Helen gathered Dallis's shawl, Rory wrote a note. He sneaked back down the stairs and into the foyer. Shaw had his coat waiting for him. Rory thanked the man and continued to his carriage, where he waited for Dallis to join him.

Well, at least Rory hoped she would.

~~~~~~

Dallis rose from her chair and went to the window to watch Rory depart. However, it was a long time before he left her grandmother's house. What had taken him so long? When he finally strode to his carriage, it was with a determination that triggered her curiosity. Was there a meaning behind his wink? Before she could react, he walked away without another glance. His behavior certainly went against the norm for the past week.

She heard tea and cake being served. Dallis held no appetite for the small repast. A tap on her shoulder had her turning to find Helen holding out her shawl.

"I thought you would feel a slight chill, my lady, from the rain."

"Thank you, Helen."

Her maid handed her the cashmere garment. Helen's hands pressed Dallis's hand into the softness. The sound of paper crinkling caused Dallis to look at Helen in askance. The confusion in her gaze prompted her maid to respond.

"A note, my lady. He awaits your answer," Helen said quietly.

Dallis slipped out the note while Helen fussed with setting the shawl around her shoulders, brushing out the wrinkles.

My dearest Dallis,

If you are as frustrated by this act of polite indifference as I am, then perhaps you would be willing to accompany me for a carriage ride. I realize my request is much to ask of you. Considering that I have done nothing but ruin you throughout our courtship.

However, I leave the choice for you to decide. If Helen opens the door, I will know that you have refused. While the loss of your companionship will affect me deeply, I completely understand. But if you do open the door, it shall bring me much pleasure.

Your devoted scoundrel,

Rory

Dallis's heart raced at his suggestion. What he proposed would be scandalous and ruin what remained of her reputation, if they were caught. But on the eve of their wedding day, she no longer cared. His note removed all her doubts on whether he wanted to marry her. It appears her scoundrel tried acting as the proper gentleman for every lady in this room. However, it was not what she wanted. She wanted the rogue who couldn't resist ruining her.

Helen whispered in her ear. "I will distract Shaw from the front door, and you can make an excuse to retrieve something from your room."

Dallis nodded at Helen's suggestion. It would appear that the lure of any attention from Roderick Beckwith would always send her to his side.

When Dallis turned from the window, everybody was enjoying their tea and cake. They discussed the flowers for tomorrow's event. She caught Kathleen's gaze and saw the laughter hidden in her depths. Kathleen's eyes were so like her brother's. A dark green that held a troubled depth but always changed to one of amusement to hide their secrets. Dallis hoped that once they were married, Rory would share his burdens—Kathleen too. Kathleen titled her head to the door with a silent message to escape. Dallis smiled in return, slipping out of the room. Her grandmother and Rory's mother were too busy with a flower arrangement to note her disappearance.

Dallis opened the door and started down the pathway to Rory's carriage. Before she could make it halfway, he flew out of the carriage and lifted Dallis off her feet, swinging her around. They laughed as the rain fell on them, soaking their clothes. Their laughter turned to passion as Rory lowered Dallis to her feet. He ran his hands through her drenched hair, lowering his head to hers. When their lips met, the desperation from being apart took hold. Dallis sighed into his kiss and melted around him. Rory pulled away.

"You came."

"Was there any doubt?"

Rory's fear kept him from answering. As he'd waited impatiently, uncertainties overtook his thoughts. With each second that ticked by, he waited in hopeful anticipation. And with every second that she didn't appear, his doubts multiplied.

Rory's look gave Dallis his answer. The whole time Dallis had feared that Rory felt trapped, he'd also experienced the same concern. Their misjudgments only confirmed her belief that they had much to learn about the other.

Rory knew that Dallis could read his thoughts. He needed to explain his behavior and hoped that she'd understand. He leaned over to place a soft kiss on her lips and led her to the carriage. Inside, Rory gave instructions to the driver to drive them around London for an hour. He yearned to spend more time than that, but Rory didn't want Dallis to suffer any more of her grandmother's disappointment.

As Rory sat across from Dallis, she suffered the same sense of loss from before. While his passionate kisses showed his true feelings, his behavior now confused her. She watched him take a deep breath, wiping his hands along his trousers, and Dallis realized he was nervous. It was endearing. Dallis settled back against the cushions, waiting for him to speak.

Rory saw a secretive smile light her face as he worked up the courage to explain himself. What went through the minx's mind? When she dropped the shawl and ran her fingertips across the opening of her dress that slid unbuttoned during their embrace, Rory gulped. When she softly spoke his name, Rory shook his head.

No, he would resist the temptation. He wanted to explain and give her the ring he'd bought. Rory wanted Dallis to wear it now. He didn't want to share the joy of the gift with the guests at their wedding.

"Rory," Dallis sighed again.

Dallis tried to lure him into more kisses and saw that teasing him was only making Rory more nervous. So she reached across and slid her fingers into his hand and offered a smile of encouragement.

He said, "While I want nothing more than to hold you on my lap and kiss your lips senseless, there is something I want to explain to you."

Dallis blushed at his blunt explanation. She hoped to provoke him with her actions, but was unprepared for his reaction. It would seem she had much to learn. She tried to pull away and Rory tightened his grip on her fingers.

Rory chuckled. While his love was a minx, she was still very innocent. He would enjoy teaching her many pleasures.

"I want to apologize for the distance I have placed between us this week."

"Why have you pulled away? Did my grandmother force your hand too soon? Have you changed your mind?

"No, my dear. I am more than ever determined to make you mine. I have kept a distance because you are too much of a temptation. On every occasion I have been in your company, I have ruined you. This week, I thought if I treated you with the respect you deserve, it would clear away any rumors clouding our marriage."

"Rory, I do not care of what anybody thinks of our marriage, with the exception of you and me. We are all that matters."

"I became aware of your unhappiness with the wedding preparations while I watched you. You should have showed enthusiasm. Instead you appeared as if you made a mistake."

"I have never felt that. I missed the scoundrel who tempted me with a passion that I wanted to explore. Instead, I now had a perfect gentleman calling on me who promised a lifetime of boredom."

Rory tugged on her hands, bringing her out of her seat. He settled Dallis on his lap.

"Boredom, you say?"

"Yes. Too proper for my taste."

"What is your taste, my Scottish minx?" Rory whispered in her ear, placing kisses along her neck.

Dallis closed her eyes as his lips caressed her skin. Her thoughts becoming distracted by his touch.

"I prefer scoundrels," she sighed.

He savored her soft moans, tempting Rory to cross over the line he'd promised he wouldn't. Just a few kisses to tide him over until tomorrow, then he would stop. But when his lips met hers it proved to be harder than he imagined.

Rory tried to resist her. While it was very honorable of him, it was not what either of them desired. His kisses held a part of himself back that she wanted—that she desired and needed. When he pulled away, a sense of loss invaded her soul. However, Dallis saw the determination in Rory's expression, and that he needed to prove something to himself most of all.

"I promise to be that scoundrel you prefer tomorrow. Now I want to be a gentleman and propose to you the way you deserve."

Rory reached inside his suit pocket and withdrew a small jewelry box. He rested the box on the seat next to him, lifted Dallis's hand and slowly pulled off her glove. Rory withdrew the ring and slid it down Dallis's finger. The small setting looked perfect on her. After placing a kiss on her finger, Rory was unprepared for what he saw. Dallis's tears scared him, but the adoration in her eyes soothed his fears.

Tears of joy floated over Dallis's cheeks as Rory slid the ring on her finger. The ring was a simple affair with an emerald surrounded by tiny diamonds. Nothing glamorous, but a true token of his affection. By all accounts, judging from the jewelry box, this was no family heirloom but one purchased just for her. The gesture overwhelmed her scattered emotions.

The highs and lows of the week took hold. She chocked back a sob when he again kissed her finger with the ring.

"Dallis, I know I have already requested the honor of you becoming my bride. While I meant every word, it was not the way I wanted to ask. Now I am asking as a man who has fallen under your spell and knows no other way to survive but to become yours forever. Will you take my hand in marriage?"

Dallis put her hands to his cheeks and rubbed her fingers under his eyes. His gaze still held a trouble he wouldn't share, but also a devotion that could only be love. Her scoundrel who had only ever ruined her, and still continued to do so, was a deeply romantic gentleman. Dallis had only one answer that would do.

"I would love to, my dear. Because, you see, while you may have fallen under my spell, I have fallen under yours and no other man will do."

Dallis finished with a gentle kiss upon his lips. Rory sighed his relief and Dallis answered his need. Her kisses remained soft and slow as she explored her desire. With his encouragement, they became bolder as their passion grew.

But before they could explore their need, the carriage came abruptly to a stop. When the door opened, they found his mother, Kathleen, and Lady Ratcliff standing outside. Dallis withdrew from his lap, wearing the mischievous smile he adored. He stepped from the carriage and pulled her out with his hands around Dallis's waist. Rory heard her grandmother's disapproving humphs as he kept Dallis close to his side.

Dallis wanted to laugh at the situation, but didn't want to make matters worse for Rory. She showed the ladies the ring. That seemed to appease them somewhat. When Rory's mother winked at Dallis, then Dallis knew that Lady Beckwith would be a strong supporter of their marriage.

Rory watched Dallis soothe the women's concerns on their scandalous outing. He knew he still needed to work on Dallis's grandmother's acceptance, but from the wink he witnessed his mother giving Dallis, he knew his mother approved. Kathleen nudged him in the side and laughed at yet another predicament he was putting himself in regarding Dallis. It was during that moment, Rory no longer cared what anybody thought. As long as Dallis stood by his side, it was all that mattered. In time, he would share his financial troubles with her.

For now, he only wished for Dallis to be happy.

Chapter Twenty

Their wedding was a splendid affair surrounded by their close circle of family and friends. Dallis was a lovely bride who made him proud. Rory only hoped he could make her just as proud. After the brunch her grandmother so graciously provided for the guests, Rory whisked Dallis away on their honeymoon. Sheffield also gifted them with one of his many carriages for them to enjoy a smooth ride. Sophia explained to Rory that the servants had prepared the home with essentials and they would have complete privacy when they arrived. A dinner would await them. The servants would come by daily to prepare meals and clean. The rest of their time they could enjoy the place to themselves.

On their ride toward Camberley, Rory smiled upon his bride who sat across from him. She smiled shyly back, wringing her hands in what appeared to be nervousness. He crooked his finger at her to join him. Dallis shook her head, which only made him chuckle. Since she wouldn't join him, then he must keep her company for the long journey.

When Rory lifted her across, Dallis let out a squeal until she settled on his lap. They sunk into the soft cushions. Rory nuzzled at her neck, and Dallis giggled. He was incorrigible.

"What is so funny, my wife?"

"Why you are, my husband."

Rory smiled and pressed his forehead against hers. "You have made me the luckiest man today."

Dallis rested a palm on his cheek. "It is I who is the lucky one."

Rory captured her mouth with a kiss built up from the passion he'd kept contained all week. Now that she was his, he could kiss Dallis at his every whim. Dallis's fingers slid through his hair, bringing his lips closer. He tried to take it slow, but soon desire overtook his rational senses. Rory devoured her lips, drinking from them like a starving man. One kiss after another, none of them enough to satisfy his thirst. Dallis's lips opened, returning his kisses with a passion of her own. She clung to him.

Dallis waited all week for his kisses. Rory had teased her throughout the season with his passion. Now she could open her arms wide. Each stroke of his tongue had Dallis whimpering for more. When he kissed her harder, she responded with her own ardor. Their arms became entangled. There was no air left between them, but still they couldn't get close enough. The clothes on their bodies were a hindrance she tried to remove, but he stopped her.

"No, my dear. As much as I desire you, I will not allow your first time to be in a carriage. No, when I make love to you it will be on a bed that you must endure for hours."

"I will endure them with pleasure," Dallis huskily replied. Which only enflamed his desire.

Rory groaned and dropped his head back against the cushion, trying to bring his body under control. They still had a few hours before they would arrive at their destination. How he would tolerate to the rest of the ride was clueless to him. Rory should return Dallis to the other side of the carriage, but her soft bottom pressed into his cock decided that he would be a fool to do that.

Dallis felt how excited Rory was with his hardness pressing against her bottom and resolved that since he'd teased her all season, she would tease him for the remainder of the ride. Twice this week Dallis had read the book Sophia loaned her. Her excitement to be intimate with Rory only grew stronger. She learned a few tricks to entice a man without him realizing it. She shifted, pretending to get comfortable, knowing that her movements would drive him crazy. She heard his groan, and watched his eyes squeezing tighter.

Next she laid her head on his chest, her fingers trailing up and down innocently, talking about their special wedding. As Dallis talked he murmured his agreement, undoing her hat and dropping the pins onto the floor, her hair flowing around her shoulders. His fingers ran through the strands, rubbing her head, and easing the tightness where her hair had been bound. She moaned and snuggled in closer, enjoying the sensation of somebody taking care of her. Before long Dallis forgot who tried to seduce whom.

When the carriage stopped and the footman opened the door, Rory looked deeply into her eyes with a sensual gaze that made her blush. For it explained his intentions for this evening. Without a single word, he carried Dallis inside the house and straight to the bedroom prepared for their stay. Soft candlelight led the way to the bedchamber where the scent of roses greeted them. Once they reached the bedroom, he closed the door and carried her toward the bed.

Rory slid Dallis down his body until her feet touched the floor. Then he proceeded to undress her. They spoke not one word. Every touch of his fingers, and the soft kisses he placed on her body, spoke volumes. When Dallis stood before him naked, the softness of his gaze spoke of a desire she was powerless to.

As Dallis stood before him, his restraint amazed him. He didn't want to rush their first time. Rory wanted to savor every touch, kiss, glance, and sigh as he loved her. She'd teased him in the carriage and he enjoyed that. There were so many facets to Dallis's character he wanted to learn.

"You, my dear, are a minx."

"How so?" she whispered.

He didn't answer her, because she began to undress him in the same slow manner. With each garment she took off, Dallis replaced them with her touch and kiss. He allowed her to explore, taking pleasure from her curiosity. She traced the firmness of his chest and along the muscles in his arms. For a gentleman of the ton, they were rough. She pressed her lips to every bit of him. Soon she brushed across his hardness. He inhaled sharply and Dallis smiled at him.

Very slowly she opened the buttons on the placket of his trousers. She knelt, dragging his pants down and off his body. As she stayed on her knees, she ran a finger along his cock. Rory hissed, tugging gently her hair. Dallis wrapped her hand around him and stroked him up and down. He was smooth and warm to her touch. As he throbbed in her hand, she wondered how he would taste. Would her kiss give him the same pleasure that she received from him? Her tongue slid along the length of him. Rory's fingers tightened in her hair as she continued to explore with her mouth. When she slid him inside her tongue twirled around in circles, Dallis felt his growl of pleasure vibrate off her tongue.

Dallis's mouth was madness. Where did she learn of this act? The way she sucked him and her tongue licked his cock, he didn't care, as long as she didn't stop. The pleasure almost brought him to his knees. She was beyond a minx. Dallis was a temptress with her long red hair and a body of Venus.

He pulled her off the floor and into his arms. Rory carried her to the bed where he laid her on the silk sheets.

This time she crooked her finger at him, and he came willingly. She opened her arms to welcome him. Her lips lifted to capture his and Dallis trembled from passion. He lifted one of her legs around his hips, searching for her need. Rory groaned into her kiss as he discovered her already wet. He slid two fingers inside her core, moving in and out as she arched her body. Her leg tightened around him and he stroked her higher.

Dallis's gripped his body as Rory brought her pleasure to a height she didn't know existed. She wanted him with a passion beyond her control. With the flavor of him still fresh on her lips, she kissed him, pleading for more. When his lips left hers, she whimpered her disappointment until he stroked her nipples with his tongue. Her whimpers soon turned into moans of pleasure. With every stroke of his tongue his finger would move in the same rhythm. Then Rory slid her nipple between his lips and sucked gently at first, teasing until the bud hardened. He sucked harder and his finger stroked faster, causing Dallis to feel as if she would explode. His strokes intensified as he sucked on her other nipple until it too hardened into a tightness. At her encouragement, he removed his hand from her core where she ached with a need.

Dallis was ready for him, from how she gripped his fingers inside her to the sweet buds he sucked on. He lifted both her breasts and caressed the globes, pinching her nipples, making her moan. Then he lowered his head taking each nipple one at a time into a gentle kiss, sliding himself inside her. Rory slowly drew out each kiss, sinking deeper into her wetness. He watched for any sign of pain, gazing into her eyes where he saw the love she never spoke aloud, and he moved past the final barrier. Dallis's body tensed for a brief second before she sighed and wrapped herself tighter around him.

The pain lasted for a brief moment. She noticed the apprehension in Rory's eyes when he pushed himself further inside her. Dallis wrapped her body around him, encouraging him to her pleasure. Once Rory saw that Dallis suffered no discomfort, he no longer held himself back. Each stroke of his body became stronger as she responded. His eyes captured hers as he made love to her. Rory lifted her leg higher around his hip, slowly sliding deep. Dallis felt him to her core. He moved quicker and rotated his hips in small circles drawing out her passion. When Dallis moved with him, he growled and his strokes became faster and stronger as he sent them exploding into a passion neither one of them imagined.

Their bodies clung tight to each other in the aftermath of their loving.

"Most definitely a minx," he whispered, pulling her closer.

Dallis smiled into his chest, realizing that he knew her tricks in the carriage and played along with her. And as she drifted asleep in his embrace Dallis realized he loved her. A man didn't make love so passionately to a woman without loving her. She had yet to speak of her love for him, still guarding her heart from pain. She didn't love easily, probably from spending most of her life unloved. Mixed emotions tried to fight their way through, but sleep prevailed.

Rory held Dallis as she fell asleep. He didn't confess his love again. He wanted to, and hopefully elicit a response, but he needed to earn her love by overcoming his previous behavior. She hadn't spoken of her love, but he believed Dallis loved him. She might not have spoken the words, but her actions betrayed her. When she was ready to speak those words, he would be ready to hear them.

For now, holding Dallis in his arms was enough.

Chapter Twenty-One

They spent two glorious weeks enjoying the comfort of Sheffield and Sophia's gift. Rory spoiled Dallis every second. They spent most of their time between the sheets, discovering the pleasures of their desires. When they weren't making love they explored Camberley and took long walks on Sheffield's estate, which was nothing less than a mansion with huge grounds.

They were returning home on the morrow and Dallis was nervous. She didn't want to step on Lady Beckwith's toes. Dallis admired the woman for raising a caring son. She hoped they could work together to make their home a loving place. She wanted to confide in Rory, but ever since they made love this morning he had been distant. Dallis hoped on their walk he would explain what was on his mind. She planned a picnic near the pond, with a basket packed with his favorite foods to entice him.

She wore a secretive smile, spreading the blanket across the ground. She talked excitedly, unpacking the contents of the basket. When she uncovered the dishes, Rory saw Dallis had included all of his favorites. Already early in their marriage she spoiled him. He only wished he could return the gesture. Rory hoped that when they returned home, Sheffield had his blunt. If not, he didn't know how to break the news to his family. They would have to sell their home. Rory could raise funds by the sale since the house wasn't entailed. For now he needed to put his worries behind and thank his wife properly. His sour attitude had put a damper on the final day of their honeymoon.

After Dallis emptied the basket, she attempted to brighten Rory's mood. However, when she looked his way he regarded her in a predatory manner. All thoughts flew from her mind when he crooked his finger. To make his point clear to her he started unbuttoning his shirt. Dallis's eyes flew around looking for any unwanted company.

"Nobody is near, Dallis."

"But they could be."

"We are on a private property in an isolated spot. Now come here, wife, before I come after you."

Dallis rose and backed away from the blanket. She wasn't as daring as her husband. His threat was viable because he rose and followed her, scooping Dallis into his arms near the pond. He dipped her low pretending to drop her. Dallis clung to his shoulders.

"You would not dare."

"Perhaps I shall. It would give me a perfect reason to get you undressed."

"Lord Beckwith, lower me this instant."

"If you insist," he said, dipping her into the pond.

He only meant to tease her enough to gain a few kisses. Rory wasn't prepared for Dallis to panic and try to crawl around his neck. Her struggles ended with both of them falling into the icy cold water. He went under as she continued to cling to him. When he finally came up for air, it was to find Dallis in tears.

"Oh darling, don't cry."

Rory carried her to the blanket. He set her on the ground, placing the dishes back in the basket. He reached for the blanket, took off her dress and his wet clothes, and wrapped it around them. Then he gathered Dallis close and held her as the chills shook her body along with her tears. He'd acted like a brute, and so hushed her with whispering endearments to keep Dallis from crying any longer. When she started to hiccup, he chuckled and leaned against the tree.

Dallis's wet chemise clung to her body causing the dampness to soak into his bones as he cuddled her closer. She squirmed in his arms causing her bottom to nestle into his cock. Soon the chill left his body to be replaced by an undeniable heat. Perhaps the afternoon would go as he planned. The dunk in the pond only a minor infraction.

Dallis was so embarrassed of how she'd caused Rory to dunk them into the pond. He was only being playful and since she didn't want to get wet, it almost caused them to drown. Her surprise ruined by her foolishness. After her tears subsided, she started to hiccup, which only caused more embarrassment. However, after a while, she realized Rory's desires had not diminished. His hardness pressed into her damp bottom. Perhaps the afternoon would go as she planned and getting wet ended up being the perfect enticement. Not wanting to let the moment slip away, Dallis trailed her fingers across his wet chest, tracing the drops of water away with her touch. When her lips followed the path, Rory moaned and pressed his hips into her buttocks, showing his pleasure. She tipped her head back to see his expression, caressing him, and was met with a stare filled with desire. He took her lips in a passionate kiss.

Rory didn't rush, only taking what she offered. They were long slow kisses which drugged his body with desire. His need to possess her was stronger than ever. He guided her body so that she straddled his legs, her core pressing into his cock. He pulled away to see her wet chemise displaying her hard nipples. The rosy pebbles showed through the garment. He brushed his knuckles across them, wanting to hear her moan. When she did, he repeated it again. This time taking them between his fingers and lightly pinching. Dallis's reaction was to press against his cock rotating her hips. His wife was a quick learner on what pleased him. Rory took her nipple in his mouth through her slip. He sucked the material, scraping his teeth across the tight bud.

"Ohhh," Dallis moaned.

Her enthusiasm fueled his desire to please her. He stripped off the wet garment and held her breasts in his hands. She arched her body as he lowered his head to taste her without the damp material in the way. If Dallis's moans made him ache before, the flavor of her on his lips made him mad. He already knew she was ready for him, her wetness coating the outside of his cock. He wrapped his arms around her waist and lifted, guiding himself inside. Rory entered slowly so they could both take pleasure of their bodies joining as one. When he fully entranced his cock, he pushed up.

Dallis's moaned in shock, her eyes wide that they would make love in this position.

"How does this feel, Dallis?"

"Ohhh." Was the only sound that came from her mouth. Rory's pleasure left her speechless.

"Do you enjoy this position?" He rotated his hips into hers.

All Dallis could do was nod. She rotated her hips and the zing that shot through her body melted her into him. When he groaned, she did it once more. His hands tightened trying to hold her still. But he was now powerless. She rose up, sliding him out from her body, then back down even slower. Dallis enjoyed the sensation so much that she repeated it.

"Dallis," he moaned.

She took pleasure in him losing control. She slid up again, only this time she lowered herself with a speed that took their breath away. Dallis felt Rory throbbing around her and wanted him to come undone. Each time she lowered, she gained speed. He began to move with her, matching each stroke harder and firmer. Her nipples brushing across his chest only intensified their passion.

Dallis lost control with him. When she tightened around his cock, Rory knew she was ready to explode. He lowered his hand between their bodies. His fingers sunk into her wetness and rubbed his thumb back and forth, meeting her strokes. Her body fell apart as he came inside her. Rory became lost in her eyes as they both succumbed to the passion which bonded them as one. He dragged her head toward him and plundered her lips. As long as Rory breathed, his need for her would never diminish. Dallis clung to him, returning his kiss.

"Rory?"

"Yes, love?"

"Mmm, just wanted to say your name."

His emotions kept him from speaking. Rory's love for Dallis grew every day to a fullness he couldn't explain. He ached for Dallis to tell him that she returned his love. Each time, their lovemaking made their bond stronger. With each kiss, touch, and whispers of conversation, he felt like Dallis had always been a part of his life. Did she care for him in the same manner? Rory always thought he was a patient man, but he'd discovered differently where Dallis was concerned. He wanted to hear those words to feel complete. But for now he would be content to hear her speak his name.

One day Dallis would tell him she loved him, and he would treasure those words forever.

Chapter Twenty-Two

They had been home from their honeymoon for a week and Rory had yet to confide in Dallis on his financial status. So far the money collectors were absent, satisfied with the deposits he put on his accounts before he left town. Luckily they didn't bother his mother. As he stood off to the side at the Kertland Ball, Rory watched his wife gush to Sophia and Sidney about their stay in Camberley. Every now and then her glance strayed toward him, where he hadn't taken his eyes off her. Dallis would blush when their gazes connected, both of their thoughts the same. He chuckled, amused that she still blushed after all the intimate things he taught her.

Sheffield came to stand beside him.

"I see that married life agrees with both of you, Beckwith."

"It would a lot more, if you had word of your ship hitting the dock."

"It hasn't yet. But I have scouts searching for the missing ship."

"Damn, Sheffield. I am barely hanging on. If I do not have payment soon, I will lose my home."

"Allow me to loan you the money."

"No, I am already in your debt for the initial investment. If your ship cannot be located, then I shall be even more so."

When Dallis glanced over to Rory, she saw him having a heated discussion with Sheffield. What did they have to argue about?

Sophia answered the question for her. "Rory invested some money with Sheffield and the ship has been lost at sea."

"How much?"

Sidney said, "Wilde said that Sheffield fronted Rory the startup fee with a payback when the investment showed a profit."

Dallis pondered how dire Rory's financial status must be for him to argue with Sheffield where anybody could hear. She wished her friends would disclose more information, but understood why they kept silent. They directed their first sense of discretion toward Rory, who had been their friend long before Dallis came onto the scene.

Throughout the week, her mother-in-law showed Dallis around her new home. During their discussion of the household routine, Lady Beckwith informed Dallis that money had been scarce since her husband had died. But Rory always managed to find coin for anything they needed. Lady Beckwith explained how Kathleen and she assisted with the chores to offset the difference. Dallis, never one to not lend a hand, helped them this week. She enjoyed learning new meals from the cook. Rory's cook was old and unable to lift the heavy pots so easily. So Dallis pitched in to make the family meals. She swore his mother and the cook to secrecy. If Rory discovered her working, he would be furious. One day, he'd caught her making scones and forbid Dallis from working in the kitchen. When she tried to explain her joy of baking, he refused to listen. He still tried to put on a front of being able to provide for Dallis in the means she was accustomed to.

Rory felt Dallis's gaze on him. She would wonder at his anger. He ran his fingers through his hair in frustration, trying to keep his temper calm. This latest setback made him desperate. Belle had sent word on a new bloke fighting tonight, if he was interested. With a dire need for money, he decided to take up the offer.

"Wilde, will you take my wife and family home?" Rory should have asked Sheffield, but his anger prevented him from requesting Sheffield's help.

"Where are you going, Beckwith?" Sheffield demanded.

"Belle's." The one word was enough of an explanation.

"Rory, you need not fight. Take my loan, I know you are good for it."

"I will make sure they arrive home safely," Wilde told him.

Wilde understood Rory's pride better than anybody. Sheffield lived an opulent lifestyle and didn't understand Rory's struggle. Everything came easy for him. Not that Wilde ever had financial problems, but he didn't enjoy the luxuries of a duke.

"Do not let pride stand in your way," Sheffield argued.

"Sometimes pride is all that a man has, Sheffield."

Rory turned to leave. He caught Dallis's gaze. He sighed, knowing he should wish her farewell, but couldn't without explaining why he needed to leave. Rory would make it up to her later. For now, he must go to Belle's and fight. With a new fighting prospect the bets would be vast and he could earn enough coin to pacify the creditors.

Dallis watched Rory leave and didn't understand why he abandoned her without an explanation. She trusted he'd made arrangements for them to make it home. She wouldn't ask his friends where he went. If this was how their marriage would proceed, then Dallis was glad she kept her feelings to herself too. When Lord Holdenburg requested her hand in a dance she accepted. Dallis missed his company.

"I see your husband has abandoned you for the evening."

"Yes, it appears he has."

"Has the gentleman still not learned what a precious jewel he now holds in his possession?"

"My husband is well aware of what he has. Only he chooses not to admire it."

"For shame. If he shall not, then perhaps I can."

"Lord Holdenburg, I am not in the mood for this flirtation you seem to want to exhibit. Should you not be focusing on your own love life?"

"Lady Dallis, I only speak as your friend. I hoped to lift your spirits, so that you will smile. When I noticed you earlier stealing glances in your husband's direction, I will admit it made me envy the bloke."

"Lord Holdenburg, forgive my harsh words. I am a trifle upset and have taken my frustration out on you instead of the man who deserves it."

"I forgive you. Can I be of assistance?"

"Dance with me and make me smile. Then tell me how you plan to pursue Lady Kathleen. She is watching us dance."

"Is she? Does she appear jealous?"

"No, I do not believe she is."

"How disappointing."

Dallis laughed at his dejected look. Why did her husband twist her in knots, but Lord Holdenburg only made her smile?

"Can I ask you a question?"

"You can ask me anything, Lady Beckwith."

"Why are you and Rory no longer friends? Lady Beckwith speaks with loving regard toward your nature, and Kathleen explained how you were the best of friends throughout school. However, you never speak to one another."

"A long story. One that involves a bet with his father that would ruin his sister, if the truth were ever revealed. I only made the bet to prevent their father from raising the stakes to another man. Rory saw it in a different light and lays the blame for his father's death at my feet."

"Why is this your fault?"

"Because I am the reason they are broke. His father bet everything he owned, and one special thing he did not. Every time he raised the stakes,

I raised them higher. He thought he had me beat, but alas I held the winning hand. Soon thereafter his father fell ill and passed away. Rory blames the result of the card game on his demise. When he came to me and demanded that I relinquish the bet, I refused."

"What were the stakes?"

"Something I have shared with only one other person than Rory and I made a promise to never disclose the information. Although one day I will, but it shall be to the person most affected."

A niggling thought formed in Dallis's mind on who he might be discussing. If Dallis was correct, then Lord Holdenburg never stood a chance with the lady he most desired no matter how much he wanted her.

"Thank you for explaining."

"My pleasure. Now, on to lighter subjects, may I pay a visit during afternoon tea tomorrow?"

"Yes, please do." Dallis laughed.

~~~~~~

Kathleen fought her jealously watching Lord Holdenburg twirling Dallis around the ballroom floor. When her new sister laughed, envy smothered Kathleen. If Rory saw them dancing, his temper would soar. Her brother usually kept a tight rein on his temper. However, Kathleen knew he wouldn't control his possessiveness with Dallis enjoying the company of any man, as innocent as it may be. She knew Dallis only regarded Lord Holdenburg as a friend, because she saw the love shine in Dallis's eyes whenever she and Rory were together. Her brother was a fool for not informing Dallis of their dire situation. Rory never discussed with Kathleen their family's financials, but she was wise enough to realize how much their life had changed since their father died. How desperate Rory became to earn them money. He didn't come home beaten, bruised, and then poured over the ledgers all because their finances were well. No, he tried to squeeze out every pence he could.

When Rory left the ball, Kathleen knew his destination. Before long Dallis would discover it too. When she did, Dallis would no longer be a happy wife.

Chapter Twenty-Three

Dallis entertained their guests with a smile pressed to her face. A smile forced, because her husband was a fool. He stayed away throughout the night and into the following day. She'd only expected Lord Holdenburg to arrive for tea, but soon their small parlor overflowed. Her grandmother arrived, as well as Sidney and Sophia. Dallis played the gracious hostess. Lord Holdenburg, the only gentleman in the room, charmed the ladies with his wit. Even Kathleen laughed at a few of his jokes. He'd noticed Dallis's worried expression and attempted to make her happy.

The long day continued with no sign of Rory, and she moved past concern to annoyance. How dare he not come home? Dallis would have been more worried, but Rory had sent a note to his mother of his delay. Not to her, but to his mother—as if he didn't have a wife.

It was time he shared his secrets with her, and a good explanation for his disappearance. Dallis wouldn't stand by and not take notice any longer. She had more than enough ample funds for them to live a comfortable life. When she wed Rory, her father endowed a small inheritance. If Rory wouldn't say which shopkeepers needed paid, then Dallis would enlist his mother's help. It was time for them to be husband and wife in the true sense, where it mattered the most. And that was with honesty.

She understood, too, that if she wanted Rory to confide his money troubles, then Dallis must say how much she loved him.

Lord Holdenburg departed and it was only a room full of ladies, gossiping and drinking tea. Dallis wished she could relax, but an uneasiness settled over her. When the door knocker echoed through the house over and over, Dallis realized she must answer it. She excused herself.

Not one but two gentlemen who appeared to be shopkeepers stood on her doorstep. When she inquired to their needs, they thrust receipts into her face demanding payment.

Dallis offered promises that Rory would call on them as soon as he returned home. Her excuses only caused them to bellow louder. When they still wouldn't leave, Dallis reached for her reticule and withdrew some bills, paying enough to appease them with a further promise that on the morrow, after she made a call to the bank, she would stop at their shops to clear any unsettled bills. Both the men, satisfied with this, changed their attitudes swiftly and treated her with the respect of the highest regard.

After she ushered them away, she turned and found Rory glaring at her from the foot of the stairs.

It would appear he had returned home without her knowledge, sneaking up the stairs to change his clothes. Now he stood angry, his fists folded tight and his mouth pressed closed. He narrowed his eyes at the purse, furious with her actions. Well good. Both of them could be angry for all that she cared. His pride was foolish. They were a family and if he was too knuckle-headed to realize that, then she no longer cared. She lifted her head regally and moved to return to the parlor. However, he stopped her progress before she could move past him. Rory reached out and gripped her arm. It wasn't painful, but enough pressure for her to take notice.

"Madam, what did I just witness?"

"I paid off your bill collectors."

"Why?"

"Because they were causing a scene and needed to be paid."

"I will take care of my own debt."

"Your debt is mine, Rory."

"No, my debt is *only* mine."

"Rory, we are a family now. Families carry each other's burdens," Dallis pleaded.

"This was the very reason why I did not pursue you. I had no means to provide for you in the way you deserved."

"So instead it was all right to trifle with my affections and ruin me?"

"Your grandmother forced my hand before I was ready."

Dallis tried to pull out of his grasp, his hurtful words bruising her heart. Rory never meant to marry her.

"Well, consider yourself unforced."

"Dallis, you do not understand."

"No, I understand very well. I married a man who held no intention to wed me, only to bed me. Then when he became trapped, he toyed with my emotions by creating a bond so powerful I could never leave him, even if I wanted to."

"Dallis," he growled.

"Rory," her voice softened. Dallis was aware her anger would solve nothing and tried gentle words. "Let me help ease your burden. I have a small savings. We can pay off your debts and fix the house."

"No." Rory's voice grew louder. "I am the man, and I will provide for my family. We will not spend your money on another item going forward. By all rights, your money is mine and I will put it into a trust for our children. If I hear or see you paying off any debts, I will make sure you never have another coin to carry." With those words he stomped away and slammed the front door on his way out.

Dallis sunk to the bottom stair, tears streaming down her face. His anger was so unexpected. She'd tried to show that she cared by offering to help his family, and he responded with cruelty. Rory's touch was what hurt the most. It was impersonal, as if she meant nothing to him at all.

"Dallis?" Lady Beckwith spoke softly at her side.

When Dallis raised her head, she saw her guests standing in the open doorway to the parlor. Rory's shouts had echoed throughout the entire house. The looks of pity were more than she could bear.

"I only wanted to help."

"I know, my dear." She urged Dallis to her feet, guiding her into the parlor. Once Dallis settled on the sofa, they attempted to ease her despair. The more she heard their excuses, the more depressed Dallis became. She cried on Lady Beckwith's shoulder, pouring out her love for Rory. Each lady held her hand offering advice. When the afternoon turned into evening, Rory still hadn't returned. Sheffield and Wildeburg arrived to escort their wives' home, and said they would search for him. Everybody tried to reassure Dallis that this behavior was normal, and it was usual for husbands and wives to fight. The making-up was the best part.

Lady Beckwith assisted Dallis to her bedroom, helped her undress and settle in bed for the night. She reached for Dallis's hand.

"Dallis, my son is a proud man who is also a fool. I only ask for you to find it in your heart to forgive him. Rory has carried an enormous burden since his father died. He wants to be a better man than his father ever was. In doing so, he has forgotten how to ask for help. I know he feels deep sorrow for shouting at you. Give him time, my dear."

Dallis couldn't answer her. She already forgave him. Only, Rory would never forgive himself. It was another thing he would let hang over his head. Until Rory opened himself to her they would always have this distance between them. When Lady Beckwith left the room, Dallis curled on her side, bringing Rory's pillow into her arms. Her tears started again and continued to flow until she fell into an exhausted sleep.

~~~~~~

Rory sat in his favorite chair and watched how peaceful Dallis rested. His anger still boiled to the surface. Not at her, never at her. Only at himself. He was more of a fool than he thought. He let his pride ruin a beautiful thing. Shame settled over him from the way he'd spoken to Dallis. What made it even worse, the parlor was full of their family and friends. So not only did he leave speaking such hateful words, they were all witness to overhear him spout off like an idiot. He would endure a lecture from every single lady. Especially from her grandmother—he could expect to be burnt to a crisp from the fire she would unleash on him. Lady Ratcliff had warned him to treat his granddaughter with care. He had failed on all accounts.

He wanted to reach out and wipe away the tears left on her cheeks, but didn't want to wake Dallis. Disgust set heavy in his soul. Rory had only returned home long enough to make sure she hadn't left him. If she had left, he didn't know what he would do. He was a selfish bastard. With one last glance in her direction he snuck out of the house again. This time he needed to lick his wounds. When he left earlier, Rory had an appointment with the family lawyer to discuss his options. With a heavy heart, he would need to sell their home. Rory found a small house on the edge of the respectable side of London for them to move into. With a tight budget, and some extra hours from Lord Hartridge, his family would survive.

He headed to Belle's. Rory no longer planned to fight, but he felt the need for a drink or two. He wanted to stay away from his club. By now Sheffield would have heard how he treated Dallis and would take him to task. He cringed knowing he deserved the lecture and probably a punch or two, but Rory wanted to avoid any such confrontation.

So instead Rory went to where everybody else escaped to. Nobody asked questions at Belle's because they were usually there to escape too.

Chapter Twenty-Four

What did one do with a freshly married, drunken earl? Belle understood why Rory stayed away from her gaming hell and brothel. She didn't want to start any rumors about him visiting her girls. She had yet to meet Lady Dallis, but her friends said that she had a heart of gold. Since Belle couldn't take him upstairs, even to her own private chambers, Rory left her with a dilemma. The man was beyond stinking drunk. Throughout the long evening he spilled his troubles. One after another into her ear. It was dangerous, the stories concerning his father. Well, it would be to anybody else, but Belle already knew the sad tale. It was a secret she'd promised to hold and never release. For it wasn't her secret to tell. If Belle was younger and Rory not married, she would have taken him to her bed. With his hair disheveled and his clothes in disarray, he painted an adorable picture. Rory reclined in a chair, wearing only his shirt and trousers. His words slurred as he muttered his love for Dallis. Her old heart strings tugged at unrequited love.

Rory had informed Belle this evening that he would no longer fight. She understood. While Belle would miss the profits from his handsome face, he couldn't hide busted knuckles from a wife. Before long Lady Dallis would inquire to his injuries. From the sound of it, the poor fool had enough troubles after his row with his wife this afternoon. Belle needed to send word to Sheffield and Wilde to collect him and return Rory home to his lovely bride.

Belle rose to instruct Ned to deliver a message just as Bruno and Magnus forced their way into the bar. She only opened the bar to the gentry, not for the hired fighters. When they spotted Rory drunk, they punched their fists into their other hand. Devious smiles lit their faces at their foe from the ring being drunk off his ass. Belle spotted trouble and called for Ned and her other guards, but they couldn't reach Rory in time.

Brutus grabbed Rory from behind, pinning his arms behind his back, and swung him around to face Magnus. The brute punched Rory in the stomach, doubling him over, but Brutus kept him standing so that he had to take the abuse Magnus threw his way. They belted punch after punch across his face. After Magnus delivered his blows, Brutus took his turn. He knocked Rory over a group of chairs, sending him flying against the wall. Brutus lifted him like a sack of flour and tossed him to Magnus, who threw him back against the wall. The whole time Rory never punched them back. He was too drunk to walk, let alone lift his arms to punch. Ned and the guards grabbed the men before they did any more damage. Belle instructed Ned to kick them out with orders to never return. Her word would spread by tomorrow and they would never find another fighting gig again. Rory wasn't a powerful man, but his friends were.

With one look at Rory, Belle's heart broke. The man was already on his last rope, now he had it pulled around his throat. The only good thing was that with him unconscious, Rory held no clue what befell him. Blood dripped from his nose, his lip was slit wide open and his eyes were already turning purple. How would Belle explain this mess to his wife? Well, she wouldn't have to—Sheffield still owed her a few favors.

When Sheffield and Wilde walked in, that was how they found him. Beaten, bruised, and sleeping off a hangover on Belle's bar room floor. She'd covered him in a blanket and watched as he slept. When her two friends arrived to escort him home, Belle described the scene. Sheffield had started laughing when he spotted Rory sprawled out drunk. His snores echoing around them. Wilde frowned at Sheffield's humor. He understood why Sheffield laughed, but he still felt sympathy for Rory.

"How priceless. The big brute has fallen," Sheffield said.

"For shame, Sheffield. Magnus and Brutus ambushed him. The man has enough troubles. How will you explain this to his wife?" asked Belle.

"I won't. Rory put himself in this mess and he will be the one to clean it up. We each had to grovel for our wife's hand for forgiveness before we married. At least he already has the ring on Dallis's finger and doesn't run the risk of her not forgiving him."

"You are heartless, my friend," Wilde muttered.

"But correct. Am I not?"

"Correct as always," Wilde agreed.

"Well, at least clean him up before you dump him off at home," Belle ordered.

"Thank you, Belle. Dallis is most worried about him. I made her a promise that I would bring him home once I found him."

"I have sent out a warning on the street about the two brutes who beat him. They are no longer welcome in my establishment. If you can spread the word, I would greatly appreciate it."

"Consider it done."

"Grab his legs, Sheffield," Wilde said, lifting Rory's arms.

Chapter Twenty-Five

Rory attempted to awaken only for his body to reject the very idea. Every bone in his body ached. His stomach wanted to revolt and his head throbbed from the mother of all hangovers. Not only that, he couldn't peel his eyes open. When he lifted his hand to his face, the stickiness of blood coated his fingers. His mouth was dry and when he tried to lick his lips, Rory winced in pain from them being split wide open. His tongue ran over the cuts, tasting dried blood. What the hell happened to him? Rory tried to recall the previous evening, but could only remember watching Dallis sleep after their fight. Then he'd headed to Belle's, where he drank a full bottle of whiskey. It was a goodbye gift from Belle for bringing her in a small fortune during his last few months of fighting. Rory remembered her understanding why he needed to cease the bouts. He pulled his eyes open and swiftly closed them. The sun shone brightly, making his head ache even more. Then he remembered. Brutus and Magnus struck their revenge. They beat him to a bloody pulp before the guards dragged them away.

"This is becoming a bad habit of yours, Beckwith," stated Sheffield.

"But then, that happens when you get twisted inside by a good woman," Wilde said.

"Where the hell am I?" Rory groaned.

"We have managed to sneak you inside your home. It is early yet and nobody is awake," answered Wilde.

"Well, then shove off."

"Not until we discuss your recent behavior," said Sheffield

"Why the hell should I listen to you?"

"Because you're walking around with your head up your arse."

"Rory, please hear us out. Then we will leave you to plead for your wife's forgiveness." Wilde tried to be more diplomatic than Sheffield.

Rory nodded, unable to do much other than roll over and hurl. Perhaps he should—on Sheffield.

"When a man falls in love, he acts like a fool. You, my friend, are a fool of all fools. I can tell you this because not long ago I was in your shoes. We both were." Wilde indicated Sheffield.

"But we saw reason and now you must do the same," Sheffield said.

"I already understand the errors of my way. It was why I drank last night. I have listed the house for sale. I plan to grovel at Dallis's feet this morning and ask for her forgiveness yet again."

"Don't be so quick to sell. My ship docked yesterday and you will have your blunt soon."

Rory sighed in relief. The news that he had been waiting for had finally arrived. But not soon enough, not before he made a fool of himself. But still, all the same, it was news he welcomed that would help ease his financial burdens. Not completely, but enough to start.

"Thank you, Sheffield."

Rory saw them to the door and climbed the stairs to his bedroom. When he opened the door, it was to find his wife the same way he left her, asleep in their bed. It appeared she'd had a restless night. The covers were all messed and tangled around her body. Even in her sleep, Dallis suffered anguish. A frown marred her beauty and this was due to—as Sheffield put it—his foolishness. When she spoke the words yesterday, Rory knew them to be correct. They were a family and family did for one another unselfishly.

Rory crawled on the bed and stared at her sleeping. His hand reached out to wipe the frown away. Dallis's eyes fluttered open at his soft touch. When she took full notice of him, her frown turned to a look of horror. Damn, he'd forgotten about the beating. He watched her panic turning to sympathy.

Dallis awoke to the sight of Rory lying in bed next to her. At least she thought the man was her husband. There wasn't one part of his face not covered in bruises. She gently touched his sores. He closed his eyes at her caress, then turned his head and placed a kiss on her palm.

"I am sorry, love, for everything I have ever said or done to you—to not make you feel as the gentle, caring lass you are."

"Rory, what happened to your beautiful face?"

"Ah, a couple of blokes I know used me for a punching bag last night."

"Did you not fight back?"

"Well ..."

"Well what?"

"I might have been a little drunk."

"A little?"

"Well, I finished a bottle of whiskey, then Belle told me that I needed to leave."

"Belle? You were with another woman?"

Tears trickled from her eyes in confusion to his whereabouts. But then Dallis held no clue on who Belle would be and about her establishment. Secrets. He had kept enough from her to last a lifetime. Not anymore. He would explain everything to Dallis and hope she understood his actions. If not, he would fight for her.

"No, love. There is no other woman, only you. Belle owns a brothel."

"A *brothel*?" Dallis's tears flowed harder, and her cries grew louder.

Damn, he was blowing this explanation all to hell.

"She also owns a gambling hall where she has a fighting ring set up. She arranges fights for men to bet on."

"And why were *you* there, Rory?" His sweet wife took a quick turn from crying to anger.

"I have spent the last few months at her establishment fighting."

"Is that the reason your hands are rough?"

"Yes."

"Why?"

Rory sighed. This was the part he didn't want to explain but had to in order to save his marriage. He rose from the bed and discarded his bloody clothes. Then he washed himself with the small basin of water. After he drew on clean clothes, he sat in his old chair.

"I know I have no right to ask, but will you join me?" he asked, crooking his finger.

Dallis sat watching Rory as he washed. She should refuse, but it wasn't what she wanted. She wanted Rory to hold her in his arms. Dallis could tell he wished to make amends and divulge his secrets. She too wanted to share her secret with him.

Last night was the longest of her life. She woke several times to see he still hadn't come home. Each time she cried herself back to sleep. The final time she awoke, he had come home. Beaten, bloody, and bruised. But home, nonetheless.

So Dallis decided to join him. Part of being married was meeting halfway, no matter who was wrong. It opened them up to forgiveness and acceptance. Dallis walked over to where Rory now held out his hand. She slid her palm into his and sat on his lap.

Rory's heart quit beating when he asked her to join him, and didn't start again until Dallis came to his side. When she slid her palm into his with trust, he wrapped her in his embrace. Holding her tightly, he conveyed his love to her. Rory needed to tell Dallis of his love before explaining the rest of his sordid story. Then and only then was he being completely honest.

"I love you, Dallis," he whispered, placing a kiss on top of her head.

"Rory …" she began.

"Hush, I need to be honest with you. Then if you care the same, you can tell me. I would not blame you, if you change your mind."

"I won't though."

"You might, and I could not bear it, if you do. My heart is already broken from the way I behaved toward you yesterday. All along you have deserved better, but my selfishness to make you my wife has brought you nothing but trouble."

"Rory …" she tried again.

He tipped her head to his and placed a gentle kiss on her mouth, wanting to savor her taste to give him courage. When she responded lightly, mindful of his split lip, his love grew stronger.

"I do not know where to begin. I guess I will start with a few years ago before you had even arrived in London. My father passed away. Not only did he die, but he left the family's coffers dry with debt owed to half the shopkeepers in London."

"He gambled."

"Yes, he not only gambled, but collected many mistresses through the years, women that he supported. My mother was kept in the dark to his activities. We all were. He covered his tracks. At home, he was a loving father. A mentor to me, he spoiled Kathleen, and to mother he was a thoughtful and caring husband who treated her as if she was the most precious gem on earth."

"Perhaps you are mistaken about his mistresses?"

"He died in the company of one in her bed."

"Oh."

"For the past few years, I have been selling assets to keep our family afloat. Still the shopkeepers keep arriving. One by one, as they did yesterday. After university, I worked for Sidney's father, Lord Hartridge. I aided him with his research projects. He knew of my family's situation and paid me for my help. During my time working for Lord Hartridge, I became acquainted with Sheffield, who was a frequent visitor at Lord Hartridge's weekly discussions.

"A year ago I found a way to earn some extra blunt. You see, I have always had a temper and whenever I got into a fight, I always won. So when Sheffield mentioned Belle's establishment, I stopped by one evening to discover what it was all about. I had heard of Belle's place, for that is where my father lost his final card game. So it went against everything I believed in to frequent the joint. But Mama and Kathleen needed to eat, and new clothes for the season. So I fought once, and then again. Then it became a normal routine to fight on a weekly basis. Soon, money came in to pay off the debt. Then my father's mistress stopped by one day when Mama was out and threatened to blackmail our family. I agreed to pay her off with one final stipend. That dipped in our pockets more than I thought.

"With the few hours I worked for Lord Hartridge, assisting on his projects, it wasn't enough. Then Sheffield approached me with a business venture and fronted me the startup fee. He only did this out of my friendship to Sophia. I never got along with Sheffield. After I beat him up for treating Sophia with the same callus regard I treated you, he did not have to help me. But we put aside our differences. My dire situation was the reason I would not court you. I tried to stay away from you. I did not want to come to you as an impoverished man, but as a man who could provide for you with the finest you are accustomed to."

"None of that matters to me, Rory."

"Shh, let me finish, love."

"Each time I was near you, I only craved more of you. Your smile, your kisses, everything about you seeped deep into my soul. I promise I never meant to ruin you. After I made the deal with Sheffield, I started to see how I could offer you more. Then his ship became lost at sea, and one thing led to another. The next thing I knew I was the luckiest bastard in the world to have you for a wife. I have let my pride stand in the way of what matters. I realized that after I left yesterday. The heartache in your eyes, when I shouted at you, haunted me. A look that I hope I never give you a reason to give me again."

Dallis turned and placed her palms on his cheeks as gently as she could and kissed his eyes. Then softly traced his lips before placing a kiss upon them. She pulled back and rested her forehead against his, staring deep into his eyes.

"I love you, Rory Beckwith. Every bit of you. The man who you were, the man you have become, and the man I will grow old with. Even the prideful, quick-temper scoundrel who seduced his way into my heart. And the same man who holds my heart as I hold his."

"Ahh, Dallis, I do not deserve your love."

"I know, but we will work on that."

Rory threw his head back with laughter. Even through their deep discussion, only his Dallis could make a quip as she did. Their life would be full of laughter. And when they weren't laughing, they would be loving each other.

"Rory, I hope I can broach this subject with you now that you have spilled your secrets. My father gifted me with a small trust fund when we got married. I want to use the money to fix the house and hire a few more servants. I want to give your mama and sister a break. Please allow me to ease this burden for you. For us."

"Dallis, there is no need. Sheffield's ship has arrived and he will have my blunt for me in a few days. If I invest it again, within a year our life will be more secure. We will put your money in a trust for our future children."

Dallis scowled. "Rory?"

"What?"

"Have you not listened to a word *you* have spoken this morning? How are we to be a true married couple, if you will not let me help carry your burdens? You are still as pig-headed as you were yesterday." She tried to climb off his lap only for him to tighten his grip and pull Dallis back against his chest.

She was correct, he still let his pride stand in the way.

He said, "Only on one condition."

Dallis stilled, hope brimming in her heart.

"That as soon we are on our feet and I have established our money to a better advantage, we return the money to your trust. Then we will transfer it into one for our children."

Dallis squealed with joy that he was open to using her money. After all, marriage was about compromise. Rory was a proud man. This way they would ease the burden of life and still allow him to provide for his family.

"Rory?"

"Yes, love?"

"Nothing, just wanted to say your name."

Rory smiled, snuggling her closer. His body ached from the pounding he'd taken, but not holding Dallis now would hurt more. As they sat in the chair, they intertwined their fingers, whispering to each other. The longer he held her, the more he wanted to show Dallis how much she meant to him.

"Dallis?"

"Yes, love?"

"I was wondering …"

"Yes?"

"Would you like to moan my name?"

"Why, Lord Beckwith, I believe I do."

"Then turn around, Lady Beckwith, so I can kiss you properly."

Dallis turned and straddled Rory's lap. She smiled mischievously into his eyes. With a quickness she didn't expect, he pulled her nightdress off. Dallis gasped as Rory made good on his promise, his lips devouring her. One kiss led to another and made her squirm on his lap. With a growl he rose and wrapped her legs around his hips, carrying her to the bed. Dallis clung to him as Rory's lips sought hers and kissed with all the passion in his soul. She matched his kiss with the same need. They were not enough though, each of them desired to become one.

"Rory," she moaned.

"Minx," he whispered, dropping her on the bed.

Dallis laughed at his playfulness, but saw it was not to last judging from the look in his eyes. Her husband was a man possessed. Those feelings brought an ache to her core. An ache only he could fulfill. She rose on her knees and helped to peel away his clothes.

"You know, husband, you should never have gotten dressed in the first place."

"I was trying to be a gentleman, wife."

"Why start now?"

Dallis slid back on the mattress and stretched out with her arms above her head. Her breasts rose high and Rory gulped, every gentlemanly thought flying out of his mind to be replaced with the most carnal images a man could possibly have.

"You have a very sassy mouth, my dear."

"Mmm." Dallis was distracted by the sight of her husband standing with not a stitch of clothing on.

Yes, her husband was a fine specimen of a man. His cock already hard for her, she slowly slid her legs apart and ran her hands down between her breasts. Rory moaned at her attentions and laid over her. When his body brushed against her, Dallis moaned her need, opening herself wider. When his hand discovered her wet, he growled his response.

All sane thoughts left behind, Rory needed her now. Later he would make love slowly and treasure Dallis as a goddess. When Dallis took the initiative and wrapped herself around him, he needed no other encouragement. Rory slid inside her fast and hard. When she moaned and arched her body, he knew he didn't hurt her, and she was begging him for more. He slowly slid out so he could feel every entire inch of her, then slid back in the same way. Dallis's nails dug into his back. Over and over he repeated this, building their need into an ache they wanted to keep enduring. Each stroke she met him, claiming more of his soul.

Dallis clung to Rory, moaning his name over and over. His kisses drugged her with his passion. Each stroke of him entering her body joined their souls. Where one of them started, the other ended. She clung tighter, her body arched, their rhythm building higher and higher. Neither of them releasing, for they never wanted to be apart. Tears slid along her cheeks as Rory made love to her. Powerful emotions devoured Dallis's soul, making her feel complete.

When Rory saw her tears he paused, afraid that he hurt her. When he gazed into her eyes and saw the love reflected, he knew they were tears of love. Rory gathered Dallis closer, his kiss gentle as he slid in and out of her slowly so they could feel everything. He pressed into her core, kissing her deeply, putting all his love and heart into his kiss and letting Dallis know she held his heart for eternity. When Dallis kissed him back with the same love, he no longer held back and came alive in her as she released around him.

He pulled Dallis to the side and kissed her tears away. No words needed to be spoken. Except for the only ones that mattered.

"I love you, Dallis."

"And I love you, Rory."

Chapter Twenty-Six

Dallis and Rory came down the stairs much later in the day—almost early evening. A blush spread across her cheeks when they sat at the dining room table to eat dinner with his mother and Kathleen. Lady Beckwith bestowed Dallis with the smile of a woman who had experienced, and recognized, the joy of a husband who doted on her. Kathleen made a quip which caused Rory to pinch her. They sat and enjoyed the meal as a family.

"Mama, Dallis has decided the house needs refurbishing and wishes your help in redecorating," Rory announced.

"I would love to assist, Dallis. It looks a bit drab, does it not?" she said, glancing at the curtains, sending a wink in Dallis's direction.

Dallis smiled and returned her wink. The previous evening they discussed Dallis's wishes. She could see Lady Beckwith enjoyed that Dallis won the fight on using her money.

"Perhaps, Kathleen, you would like to join me tomorrow for a visit to the seamstress? And you too, Mama."

"I am sorry, Dallis, but no. I hold no coin for new dresses."

"You do now, sister," Rory told her.

"How?"

"Do not worry how. Please show your gratitude and accept Dallis's invitation."

Kathleen smiled with glee at being able to purchase new gowns for the season. Even though the season was half over, there remained enough time to make a certain gentleman take notice. Enough notice, she hoped, to pull him into her trap.

"Yes, Dallis. I would enjoy receiving some new dresses."

"Excellent, we shall make a day tomorrow of shopping, ladies. I hope you can part from me for a few hours, Rory."

"I believe I shall join you. It is not every day a gentleman can take pleasure with his family."

Dallis smiled across the table at Rory with love as his mother and sister chatted gaily of what they should change first in the house. Kathleen shared with them about a dress she saw in a shop window, and the perfect bonnet to match. Rory returned Dallis's smile with the corner of his mouth twitching in laughter. All along he had been a fool to let pride stand in his way. When, if he would have trusted in the love he held for Dallis to prosper, he could have enjoyed this sooner. Rory had wasted precious time. Not anymore though. No longer would he let his pride rule any decisions he would make for their family.

Dallis never thought she'd have the love she shared with Rory. Throughout her life, her parents left her alone and feeling unwanted. Rory made her feel whole. She knew in her heart that their love would only grow as the years passed them by. To have held onto her love and not tell Rory would have been selfish in its own right. Now, a day would never go by that she wouldn't share her love with him. Even if she had to tell him all day long, so he would never hold a doubt to her true affections.

Rory sent her a wink and nodded toward the door. Dallis shook her head and blushed the beautiful shade of red she always did when he suggested something inappropriate. He caught his mother's eye, and she smiled her approval at his choice in a bride. When she lifted her hand and shushed him away with a wink, Rory knew his mother understood what he tried to suggest to his wife. With a laugh he strolled to the doorway and stopped.

When his wife frowned at him, Rory crooked his finger. She remained in her seat, and Rory chuckled, walking to her side. Lifting Dallis from the chair he kissed her, letting everybody know his intentions. She wrapped her arms around his neck and kissed him in return.

Before Dallis could feign further protest, Rory had climbed the stairs and entered their bedroom. With slow steady kisses he made love to her throughout the night and well into the next morning.

The shopping trip the ladies planned was postponed for another day.

Epilogue

Rory's eyes drifted across the ballroom until he located his sister dancing
with another suitor. He smiled, watching the enjoyment grace Kathleen's
face. Finally, their family had settled into happiness. He wrapped his arm
around Dallis tighter, drawing her closer. His hand rested across her
stomach. If it wasn't for her love, Rory didn't know how he would have
kept enduring his father's shame. Because of her, Rory rose above the
mistakes he'd claimed as his own. He lightly traced a path back and forth
across Dallis's stomach.

Dallis shifted her attention away from their friends when Rory's
touch changed. His gentle caress across her stomach caused her to raise her
eyes to Rory's. Rory's secretive smile revealed that he'd guessed. She'd
hoped to tell him after the ball.

Rory whispered in her ear, "Would you like to dance, Lady
Beckwith?"

"I would love to, Lord Beckwith."

Dallis placed her gloved hand in his as he led them onto the
ballroom floor. Ever since they'd married, he made sure they danced at
every ball. Rory claimed he had a lot of dances to catch up on. Every dance
held a special place in her heart. This one would hold the most precious of
memories.

"Have I told you how much I love you this evening?" Rory asked.

"You have, my dear. But I never tire of hearing your sweet words."

"Do you have any news you would like to share with me?"

"Mmm. I have already told you of my love for you earlier. So that is not it. Let me see. You are not so vain as to have me speak of your handsomeness."

"Dallis," Rory growled.

Dallis laughed. This brought the eyes of the other dancers onto them. His mischievous minx was tormenting him by withholding what he desired to hear.

"I would tell you our wonderful news, but it seems you have already guessed."

"Do you not think that I don't know every inch of you, or how your body reacts to my touch? You are the other half my soul, my love. Every change in you is a change in myself. Are you …?"

Rory brought their dance to a halt. He cupped Dallis's face and lowered his forehead to hers. When tears of happiness filled her eyes, and she whispered yes, his heart filled with even more tenderness. He brushed his lips across her, kissing her *yes* into his soul. Looking up, he found them the center of attention. He laughed and twirled Dallis around, her laughter mingling with his. It would seem they were still on the tongues of the ton's gossipers. Rory no longer cared as long as Dallis remained at his side.

Dallis's love for Rory kept growing. His excitement at becoming a father was endearing. As he twirled her around, her eyes never left his. The love that shone there completed her. All her life she'd dreamed of love and now shared it every day with Rory. Dallis treasured Rory with her heart and soul.

Rory told her, "You have made me the happiest man, my dear."

"I love you, Roderick Beckwith."

"And I love you, Dallis."

Their friends and family surrounded them. Their news had spread and the well-wishers offered their congratulations.

All except for one man.

~~~~~~~

It was time to play his marker. He had waited long enough. She was his, and he would stake his claim before the week ended. For weeks now, he'd observed her charming every eligible bachelor night after night. Well, no longer. When he stated his intentions, he realized the drama that could unfold. She had been his since the moment he became aware that she was no longer a little girl, but a woman meant for his desires. He'd fought to gain her, before her father traded her for a chance at a win. The old man lost more than a card game. He lost all. Every ounce of self-respect.

His old friend, Rory, misunderstood his intentions, however Holdenburg no longer cared. He'd tried to explain his reasons, but all he ended up with was a black eye and busted fingers. Rory had crushed his hand, thinking that would change the course of the card game. But it only brought about the loss of a friendship. Lady Beckwith knew the consequences of that night and understood his reason. She had watched him enough around Kathleen to realize his true feelings for her daughter. Lady Beckwith encouraged Holdenburg to pursue Kathleen, but she rebuffed him at every effort. Well, now she no longer could. Soon. It was only a matter of time.

Kathleen saw him out of the corner of her eye. As she stood with her family enjoying Rory and Dallis's wonderful news, her pull toward Holdenburg never wavered. In turn, Lord Holdenburg's eyes never strayed from her throughout the evening. Why did he regard her with such intent? He'd not danced with anybody at the ball, only watching her from the balcony. He nursed one drink all evening, not conversing with a soul.

Kathleen had sensed the first shiver of his attention and the hair rose on the back of her neck. When she glanced around, Kathleen found him regarding her with an air of possessiveness. Each dance around the floor brought her within inches of him and his intent. Even now, as Kathleen stared back at him, Holdenburg intrigued her like never before. She didn't understand. Over the last few years, the only emotion Lord Holdenburg invoked in Kathleen was hatred. When it changed, she didn't know. It was only when Mama urged him to court Dallis did Kathleen feel the small tug of jealously. Which was ridiculous.

When her gaze entangled with his, his smile took on a predatory grin. Holdenburg lifted his glass to Kathleen. In an acknowledgement of what, she held no clue.

~~~~~~~

Read Kathleen & Holdenburg's story in The Scoundrel's Wager

Visit my website www.lauraabarnes.com to join my mailing list.

"Thank you for reading I Shall Love the Earl. Gaining exposure as an independent author relies mostly on word-of-mouth, so if you have the time and inclination, please consider leaving a short review wherever you can."

Author Laura A. Barnes

International selling author Laura A. Barnes fell in love with writing in the second grade. After her first creative writing assignment, she knew what she wanted to become. Many years went by with Laura filling her head full of story ideas and some funny fish songs she wrote while fishing with her family. Thirty-seven years later, she made her dreams a reality. With her debut novel *Rescued By the Captain*, she has set out on the path she always dreamed about.

When not writing, Laura can be found devouring her favorite romance books. Laura is married to her own Prince Charming (who for some reason or another thinks the heroes in her books are about him) and they have three wonderful children and two sweet grandbabies. Besides her love of reading and writing, Laura loves to travel. With her passport stamped in England, Scotland, and Ireland; she hopes to add more countries to her list soon.

While Laura isn't very good on the social media front, she loves to hear from her readers. You can find her on the following platforms:

You can visit her at *www.lauraabarnes.com* to join her mailing list.

Website: **http://www.lauraabarnes.com**
Amazon: **https://amazon.com/author/lauraabarnes**
Goodreads: **https://www.goodreads.com/author/show/16332844.Laura_A_Barnes**
Facebook: **https://www.facebook.com/AuthorLauraA.Barnes/**
Instagram: **https://www.instagram.com/labarnesauthor/**
Twitter: **https://twitter.com/labarnesauthor**
BookBub: **https://www.bookbub.com/profile/laura-a-barnes**

Desire other books to read by Laura A. Barnes
Enjoy these other historical romances:

<u>Matchmaking Madness Series:</u>
How the Lady Charmed the Marquess
How the Earl Fell for His Countess
How the Rake Tempted the Lady
How the Scot Stole the Bride
How the Lady Seduced the Viscount

<u>Tricking the Scoundrels Series:</u>
Whom Shall I Kiss... An Earl, A Marquess, or A Duke?
Whom Shall I Marry... An Earl or A Duke?
I Shall Love the Earl
The Scoundrel's Wager
The Forgiven Scoundrel

<u>Romancing the Spies Series:</u>
Rescued By the Captain
Rescued By the Spy
Rescued By the Scot

Printed in Great Britain
by Amazon